D0984927

RED RIVER COUNTRY

Center Point
Large Print

**This Large Print Book carries the
Seal of Approval of N.A.V.H.**

RED RIVER COUNTRY

E. E. Halleran

CENTER POINT LARGE PRINT
THORNDIKE, MAINE

This Center Point Large Print edition
is published in the year 2014 by arrangement with
Golden West Literary Agency.

The text of this Large Print edition is unabridged.
In other aspects, this book may vary
from the original edition.
Printed in the United States of America
on permanent paper.
Set in 16-point Times New Roman type.

ISBN: 978-1-62899-151-2

Library of Congress Cataloging-in-Publication Data

Halleran, E. E. (Eugene E.), 1905–
  Red river country / E. E. Halleran. — Center Point Large Print edition.
    pages ; cm
  Summary: "A Texas Ranger and his scout enter the dangerous Red
River area to stop gunrunners from selling to Indians and must deal with
others who want the guns for themselves"—Provided by publisher.
  ISBN 978-1-62899-151-2 (library binding : alk. paper)
  1. Texas Rangers—Fiction. 2. Large type books. I. Title.
  PS3515.A3818R43 2014
  813′.54—dc23
                                                                    2014012980

RED RIVER COUNTRY

Chapter 1

The Red River looked as if it properly deserved its name when Hale and Tolliver halted on the ridge. Patches of Indian paintbrush flamed in the May sunset and even the brown mudflats along the meagre trickle of water had taken on some of the ruddy glow of the western sky. Lengthening shadows in their dark contrast only seemed to accent the redness of everything.

"Still enough light for a quick look," the tall man said without turning in the saddle. "You'd better find something here or I'll be tempted to try hammering the truth out of you." The words were grim but the tone was vaguely good-natured. There was even a pucker of amusement in the sandy stubble around the tight lips.

Old Ben Tolliver grunted, a bob of the grizzled head jamming a gray beard a little more snugly against the thin chest. Ben was hunched, scrawny, gnarled, tough, and shrewd. At the moment he was too shrewd to get into any argument with Tom Hale about truth. Hale had been openly skeptical from the beginning and the past two days of fruitless searching had not helped any. "There's gonna be sign, all right," Ben assured him. "Gotta be. Mellew had to come this way and he shore as hell musta got this fur by now."

"So you keep telling me."

"We missed him, that's all. We cut across that big loop o' the Red and I don't reckon as how he'd know about the shortcut. Musta follered the river all the way."

"Start looking. I want sign—not explanations." Then he settled his lean length a little more comfortably in the saddle and added, "I'll take that extra bronc you're leading."

Tolliver was still muttering as he reached back to unfasten the lead rope. "Gonna find tracks this time, Cap'n. Don't ye fret about it. Mellew had to use this side o' the Red. He couldn't risk gittin' mixed up with them outlaws over in the Nations— and he shore as hell didn't ride east. Yank patrols is coverin' that country like a swarm o' locusts." He passed the rope to Hale and the tall man took it without comment, knotting it loosely to the thongs that held his slicker roll behind the saddle.

Old Ben grinned as he kneed his horse down the slope toward the bottom lands and Hale knew what the grin meant. Ever since their meeting on the Washita, the old man had been trying to trick his former commander into old habits. Now he had done it. The business of turning extra horses over to Hale while Tolliver hunted sign was something straight out of a happier past. Obviously the old man was pleased.

A moment of mild amusement passed as Hale eased his bronc down the grade but then some of the old resentment stirred in him. He could appre ciate the way old friends had tried to stir him ou of the lethargy he had brought back from th Union prison camp, but he had done little to hel himself. Mostly he had been annoyed by the well meant efforts, stubbornly preferring to nurse hi grudge. With Ben Tolliver he couldn't do it. Ber might be a thorough scoundrel in many ways bu he was loyal to Tom Hale. He might lie—anc generally did—but he would be dependable in a pinch.

Hale shoved the thought aside, recalling tha holding horses was not his only chore at a time like this. Ben had to be covered while he looked for trail sign. Out here at the edge of outlaw country it didn't matter very much whether Tolliver had lied or whether he hadn't; the danger was present and it was up to Hale to protect his friend.

The younger man took his post on the lower slope. From that point he could keep a wary eye on the winding line of cottonwoods that separated bottom lands from mudflats. A little less distinctly he could trace another line of cottonwoods which separated the mud from the lush greens of the north side. That was really the danger area. Over there was the Nations, hangout of the border's worst.

He sat up a little straighter in the saddle as he estimated distances. Ben was probably safe nough from any sniping attack from the far shore ut Hale didn't relax. He even felt pretty good to e working this way with Old Ben. It would be nteresting to see how this thing was going to turn ut. Tolliver's crazy schemes usually had something back of them.

When he was certain that no hidden enemy urked anywhere among the willows, he rode on lown to where Tolliver was scurrying around in he dusk. Evidently Ben had found some sort of a trail, so Hale simply waited, keeping the norses away from any sign which still required attention.

"What luck?" he called out when Ben straightened up from his work.

The gray head swiveled. For Ben Tolliver it was easier to turn his head than to lift it. "Two wagons," the old man reported. "One of 'em could be Chris Mellew's outfit. Right size fer a Dougherty wagon."

"Two wagons!" Hale repeated. "I thought you were sure that this was a one-wagon operation."

"That's how it started. Could be there was more to it than I knowed about. Or mebbe somebody else got on Mellew's trail."

"Why should they?"

"Lots o' reasons. Mebbe some other lawman got wind o' what was goin' on. Mebbe Stiles coulda found somebody else he could trust and sent 'em out from Austin. Mebbe bandits figgered to steal

the guns. Stuff like that oughta fetch a right fai
price over in the Nations."

"You'd know all about that, I suppose?"

Tolliver chuckled. "Now ye're soundin' like ol
times, Cap'n. Makin' out I'm a crook."

Hale joined in the laugh. It was hard to sta
stern with Old Ben. "Get honest for a minute," h
urged. "Did you have any notion that Mellev
would find anybody on his trail but us?"

"Not fer sure—but it ain't hard to figger. Lik
the Good Book says, Woe to the evil man fer hi
enemies is too many to git counted.' Coulda beer
plenty fellers what knowed about the deal anc
might try to grab a hand."

The week's growth of sandy whiskers puckerec
comically as Hale begged, "Please don't star
any of your quotations, Ben. I'd rather listen tc
your lies. One's about as honest as the other." He
didn't sound as rough as he wanted to. Anyway, i
wouldn't have done any good. Ben had heard the
complaint too many times in the past. Once in a
while some bit of Tolliver philosophy would come
out reasonably like the true version, but mostly
there would be a twist in it that was strictly
Tolliver. Anything that appealed to the old man as
good sense would be offered as a famous remark,
usually with the credit assigned to Holy Writ or tc
Ben Franklin. Tolliver didn't seem to think much
of other sources.

"Gittin' to sound more and more like yerself,"

Ben cackled. "Always raisin' hell with me about somethin'." He seemed quite delighted.

"Likely I'll raise more with you before this is over," Hale told him. "I don't know why Headley Stiles took a chance on putting a message into your crooked clutches—except that he knew you'd find me—but I'm betting that you've found some way to mess it up for your own purposes."

"Cap'n, I swear . . ."

"Don't bother. I'll find out soon enough. Meanwhile there's a job to do. Tell me what you could figure out from the sign—and make it as honest as your sinful nature will permit."

Ben grinned at his tone but then sobered. "It's got me puzzled a mite, Cap'n. Chris Mellew started out with one wagon. Now there's two of 'em."

"Maybe that's reasonable enough. I never could put much stock in a tale about one man hauling so many stolen muskets in one light wagon."

"Somehow it don't add up," Tolliver growled, ignoring the continued hint that he had not told the truth about the affair. "Looka here, Cap'n. Ye kin see what I'm gettin' at." He made a show of pointing to the trampled grass where the fading red light showed wheel marks. "These marks was made by a light wagon like the one I seen Mellew fixin' up—or gittin' fixed up. Now, look here. Broad tires. Heavy. This wasn't no Dougherty wagon. And it went through ahead o' the ambulance. Ye kin see the narrer track on top o' the wide one."

"Then the big wagon wasn't chasing Mellew? Is that the idea?"

"Right. And the big outfit had an ox team. That ain't the kind of a rig to do no chasin' with. Anyhow it went along fust."

"You're sure the light one was Mellew's? Plenty of ambulances around since the Yanks took the Mississippi and kept us from sendin' 'em across."

"Light wagon and a mule team. That's all I know. It's the right combination to be Mellew— and it ain't too common in these parts. I'm bettin' it's him."

"A big wagon still sounds more like what would be used to haul a load of guns. How long ago did they pass here?"

"A day. Mebbe less. While we was ridin' east on the shortcut they musta been follerin' the river west. Do ye think we oughta cut back across or keep to their trail?"

"I think we'll stick with their trail. I'm getting mighty curious about a lot of things."

The gray beard swung in an arc as the old man turned his head on his scrawny neck. "Reckon ye're right. And ye're thinkin', Cap'n. Good."

"Shut up! If I was doing any real thinking I'd be trying to figure out what kind of a lie you must have told me."

"Ye hurt me, Cap'n. But let's git movin'. There's

13

bit o' light left so I'll see about trackin' these wagons a mite."

Hale nodded and took his horses back to higher ground. There he halted, once more alert to possible danger from the opposite shore. The Red wasn't much of a river at this time of year. It wouldn't serve as any real barrier against the assorted thugs who had haunted its north bank since the beginning of the big war. Neither the Union nor the Confederacy had had the men or the inclination to do anything about this wild border country, so the Nations had become more than a mere land of savage tribes. The Indians were not nearly as savage as the renegades, deserters, runaway slaves, and assorted outlaws who took refuge there.

Hale had been carefully briefed on the region before he was sent out to the Washita with the Confederate Peace Commissioner who was supposed to set up a peace treaty between the Confederacy and the various Indian tribes. Texas was particularly interested in such a treaty, so they had wanted someone with the party who would understand Texas concerns. Also they wanted to do what they might to avoid having the peace party run into trouble on the trip up the Red River. Hale had been picked for the duty.

Headley Stiles had overruled Hale's objections, arranging for the returned prisoner to be ordered back into Ranger service. It was easy to ignore the fact that there had been no Ranger battalion in Texas since the entire force had been mustered into Confederate service at the beginning of the war. The terms of Hale's parole as an exchanged prisoner would not stand in the way of such service and the expedition would permit a quick survey of the country which might offer the best route for further cattle drives.

Hale hadn't argued very hard. He didn't care one way or another. He was still brooding over the way his war affairs had gone and he didn't even bother to comment on the commission Stiles secured for him. It didn't seem important. Becoming a Ranger Captain wasn't much of an honor when the title was being conferred by a government that might find itself out of business before the current duties could be performed.

The peace group had been duly escorted to the Washita where several thousand Indians of many tribes had gathered for the occasion. The journey had been uneventful. No outlaw trouble had developed along the Red or on the ride north across to the Washita. Then Tolliver had appeared with the message about a plot to run guns to somebody, presumably warlike Indians. Headley Stiles had supplied little information, only that several hundred muskets had been stolen from a temporary arsenal in eastern Texas and were believed to be on the way to outlaws—red or white—in the Indian Nations. It had been Tolliver who had provided the dubious facts regarding one Chris Mellew.

Hale was reviewing the whole story in his mind as they rode up the river a short distance before making a quick camp in a pecan grove. He knew that bitterness had kept him from giving the tale proper attention, but now he felt his interest rising sharply. He liked it that way. The months of bitter resentment toward the people responsible for the war had not been good for him. He felt better simply to have a job ahead that needed doing.

When he issued crisp orders about the night camp he could see that Ben was pleased. The old man had been trying pretty hard to stir up exactly that kind of change.

They turned in without any fire, but at dawn they took a chance on one, boiling their coffee under cover of a river fog which blanketed the whole valley. Long before the morning mists cleared, they were riding once more, this time on the ridge instead of down in the bottoms where the wagons had moved.

"We can't afford to blunder into anything in the fog," Hale said by way of explanation. "Plenty of time to check sign after we have a little better chance to see what's around us. You take the lead; I'll bring the horses."

Tolliver's lean features wore a happy grin as he obeyed orders. Hale wished that he knew what the grin really meant. Probably Old Ben was happy to see his old commander acting like old times—but maybe he was also gloating over the way some scheme was working out. There was a scheme, of course. With Ben Tolliver there was always a scheme.

Hale went over the details in his mind, trying to give them a little more attention than he had done earlier. The message from Headley Stiles was authentic enough. Stiles was not only the state official who had arranged for the Washita trip and the Ranger commission, but he was also the man who was to be Hale's partner in that cattle driving business they were planning. Like Hale, Stiles would have had a double motive for trying to stop gunrunning. A good peace with the Indians was important to the Texas border and important to the plans of future drovers. And Stiles would have known about Ben Tolliver, would have trusted him to get through to the Washita with a message for Tom Hale. Up to that point everything seemed right. The doubt centered around Old Ben's statement that the guns were being hauled up the valley of the Red in one small wagon by a man named Chris Mellew. Maybe that second wagon was part of the answer.

Two hours later they began to move across flatter country, the ridge disappearing as bottom-lands seemed to spread out for miles on either side of the river. Cottonwoods along the mud flats offered the only cover, so they began to follow the wagon trail directly. Within minutes of the shift, they found signs of a camp. Tolliver studied the spot for a few minutes and then turned to remark dryly, "Pride goes before a fall and a haughty speerit before a red face—or somethin' like that. Looks like the Good Book had it right. I was wrong with what I told ye last night."

Hale nodded. He wasn't as good as Tolliver but he could read sign pretty well himself. "This wasn't last night's camp, was it?"

"Nope. Two nights ago. They're more ahead of us than I figgered."

"So wipe the red outa your ears and look some more. Maybe we can learn a little more about them." He turned to take the horses back out of the way.

There was no sign of movement anywhere along the river, but he kept careful watch, knowing that the valley was now clear of mist and that an enemy might spot them from a considerable distance. Old Ben worked out the sign for perhaps twenty minutes and then Hale saw something moving well down the river.

"Let's go, Ben," he called promptly. "Stay behind the trees and we'll make for that next rise that has the timber on it. Somebody's on the river trail behind us."

He took the horses directly across the sign of the wagon camp, hoping to confuse his own tracks with those already there. Maybe these newcomers down the river were not involved in any of this gunrunning business but it was best to take as few chances as possible.

They found decent cover in time to study what they could now make out to be a wagon. Both of them were quickly aware that this was one of the utility vehicles commonly called ambulances in the army but generally known as Dougherty wagons among ranchers.

"Two men, both ridin' the wagon," Tolliver murmured. "Extry hosses trailin' along behind."

"I can see. I can also see somebody across the river. Try your sharp eyes on that bare spot where the cottonwoods don't grow."

Even as he spoke he could see two riders coming out toward the mud flats on the north shore. One of them halted on solid ground but the other rode forward as though testing the consistency of the drying mud. When his horse sank to the fetlocks he backed off in a hurry and rejoined his companion.

"Seems like they want to git over to our side," Tolliver commented. "Must be that Chris Mellew's gittin' a lot o' folks interested in him."

"Then we'd better get ready for a bit of trouble. I don't think they'll try a crossing here but there's a ford not many miles upstream. I remember seeing it when I went up with the peace party."

"That ain't good," Ben muttered. "If'n the word's got out around outlaw country that

Mellew's makin' a move we're likely to find a whole passel o' hard cases tryin' to git into the game."

"Having been the first hard case to get on the trail I suppose you're jealous?" Hale mocked.

Tolliver aimed a crooked grin at him. "Cap'n, ye keep tryin' to make me out a real scoundrel."

"Wrong. I'm just trying to keep in mind that you try to make yourself out something like that. Are you telling me that a lot of people want to steal these stolen guns from Mellew?"

"I dunno what the hell they want. All I know is that we'd oughta git along to that ford ye mentioned. Things ain't shapin' up to be nothin' but a mess."

Chapter 2

They kept to the timber south of the ridge as they moved up-river, leaving the wagon trail in order to avoid being seen by either of the two lots of newcomers. Within a mile they found better country for their purpose and Hale led the way back to the ridge top. "What did you learn from the sign back there?" he asked when they had time to stop and talk.

"A couple o' things. Fust off, it don't look like Chris Mellew's in no trouble with that other wagon outfit. They musta jest happened along and he caught up with 'em."

"You're sure it was not a planned meeting? Another wagonload of guns ahead of him, perhaps?"

The old man quirked a grin at him. "Cap'n, ye know damned well I can't tell fer sure about a thing like that. All I know is that both outfits seemed to be gittin' along real good. Camped together and et together."

"How many people?"

"Four, countin' Mellew. Anyhow, four lots o' foot signs. Mellew's kinda stocky but not big, they tell me. I never seen him, ye know. There's two lots o' bootprints back there what's right fer a medium size jigger. Then there's some o' the

21

biggest damned footprints I ever seen. And a woman." He let the final words come out with an air of intentional drama.

Hale didn't even look around. "Three people in the big wagon?" he asked quietly.

"Looks thataway. I couldn't tell fer sure because none of 'em slept on the ground. I'm guessin' that Mellew's alone."

"He *was* alone," Hale corrected. "Now there's the big wagon crowd and us. Coming up fast is two more lots of company, one on each side of the river. This valley's getting to be practically crowded."

"Bound to happen," Tolliver said. "What was happenin' wasn't no secret. Lots o' fellers mighta got on to Mellew's scheme and figgered to git some o' the profits. When there's sugar ye got to expect flies."

"Ben Franklin?" Hale inquired solemnly.

"Mebbe. I dunno."

"Good stand of timber just ahead. I think maybe we ought to forget about locating that ford and see what kind of outfit is coming up this side of the river."

He swung into a convenient thicket and slid from the saddle. Old Ben followed his lead and the pair of them pushed through to a spot where they could see the whole breadth of valley without showing themselves. Hale pulled off the campaign hat and wiped sweat from his broad

22

forehead and heavily tanned neck. "Getting hot," he observed. "Maybe in more ways than one."

Tolliver was staring at the black hat as though seeing it for the first time. "Where'd ye git that fancy hat, Cap'n?" he asked. "It looks like somebody took a Yankee general's headpiece and sewed a Texas star on it in place o' the reg'lar thingamajigs."

"That's exactly the way it worked—although I don't guarantee that it was a general who lost the hat. Stiles wanted me to look official when he sent me out with the Commissioner—and don't try to change the subject. I'm still waiting to hear the real truth of this deal. You didn't tell it yet, you know."

Old Ben went down on his stomach to peer out between bushes. "That's kinda mean talk, Cap'n," he complained. "Do ye shore enough figger I'd lie to ye?"

"You always did."

This time there was no reply and Hale let it go. Ben could get pretty stubborn at times.

Within minutes they could see the wagon coming up their side of the Red. The two men on its seat seemed dusty but somewhat better dressed than most travelers in this part of the wilderness. The smaller man handled the reins of a team of well-matched grays, while another pair of similar horses trotted along behind. The wagon itself was one of those utility vehicles generally called ambulances but used by both armies for all sorts of purposes.

"Another damned Dougherty wagon!" Tolliver grunted. "Likely outa that same batch what got tied up when the Yanks grabbed the big river. That's where Mellew got his'n."

Hale's voice took on a new note as he commented, "So maybe the gunrunning business sounds a little better. I never did think much of a tale about one small wagon hauling all those muskets."

"That's the trouble. Ye didn't believe me."

"Naturally. You're such a liar that I . . ."

"Cap'n, that ain't very friendly."

"And don't try to sound hurt. The point I'm getting at is that I know that little fellow driving the wagon. With him in the picture a gunrunning yarn begins to make sense."

Tolliver laughed. "Which makes it kinda funny. I was jest makin' up my mind that I knowed the other jigger. Who's the little one?"

"His name is Garnsey. Seymour Garnsey. Ever hear of him?"

"Somebody in gov'ment, ain't he?"

"Partly. He's held a couple of posts for the Confederacy but mostly he's an off-stage operator. Army contracts and things like that."

"Ye think he might have a hand in gunrunnin'?"

"Likely enough. Back in sixty and sixty-one he was one of the loudest howlers for secession. He

24

was one of the hotheads who called Sam Houston a traitor for siding with the Union. Garnsey's a troublemaker and always was one."

"Then ye figger there might be somebody big tryin' to git guns to the Injuns?"

"It could be just that way. Maybe you didn't hear any of the talk back in Austin but there was a rumor that some of the die-hards wanted to turn this Indian confab into an alliance against the Union. The idea was that if a lot of redskins could be turned loose against Union settlements between the Arkansas and the Platte it would force the Yanks to send troops out there. That would relieve the pressure on our armies in the east."

"What armies?" Tolliver asked sourly. "The Yanks have had the Mississippi tied up fer more'n a year. Sherman has knocked the livin' hell outa Georgia and is doin' the same thing fer the Carolinas. The last I heard Lee was still holdin' out near Richmond but it wasn't likely he could stick it much longer. Likely enough he's done by this time. The damned war's over!"

"Garnsey and his gang won't admit it. That's the whole trouble."

Tolliver shook his head. "It don't look good, Cap'n. That lanky gent on the wagon with him might jest be mixed up in somethin'. His name's Jakes—or somethin' like that. He was snoopin' around Galveston when I was keepin' an eye on the way that Mellew wagon was gittin' fitted up.

Kinda sounds like things is fittin' together a mite."

"Even your story begins to sound better," Hale conceded. "Which is pretty surprising."

They watched until the ambulance disappeared around a bend where willows screened the river, then they went back to their horses and set up a few plans. Tolliver was to trail the wagons as long as there was cover to hide him from the men on the north bank. Hale would ride the ridge. For a few hours, at least, they would forget about that dangerous spot at the ford. Enemies might cross there but the first item of business was to learn more about the people who were on the south side.

Hale tried to work things out as he rode along. The sun was hot enough to make the sweat run, but he ignored his discomfort when he realized that he was following a fresh trail. A horse had walked along the ridge in the direction he was taking and he guessed that someone from the Mellew party had begun to scout the river as the wagons moved westward. Maybe that threat from the north bank had not gone unnoticed. Which meant that there must be more than two riders over there. The pair he had just seen would be miles behind the Mellew wagon.

He found where the other rider had dismounted, clearly for the purpose of using a pecan clump for extended observation of the valley. Hale did the same thing but could see no one except Ben Tolliver. The tracks showed plainly and he guessed that this must be one of the travelers Ben had described as being of medium size.

The balance of the day brought no new information and in the afternoon it was difficult to do any real scouting, the country once more opening up so that both Hale and Tolliver had to get back away from the river. It was not until just before dusk that they struck another of those lateral ridges that shaped so much of the valley. When they moved in to use the terrain for their own purposes they saw that they had made the shift at exactly the right time. The wagons were camped just ahead of them.

At a distance, and with fading light, it was difficult to make out details, but Hale counted five figures working around the wagons, evidently getting settled for the night. All of them appeared to be men.

"Looks like them last two made good time and j'ined up with the others," Old Ben commented. "Looks like mebbe the woman ain't wantin' to have 'em spot her. She ain't showin' none."

"Let's move on upstream while there's still light," Hale said. "I'm not as much interested in the woman as I am in finding that ford I mentioned. It can't be far away and it might turn out to be important."

He was turning his horse when Tolliver exclaimed, "Damnation! That ain't Mellew's wagon!"

"What do you mean?"

"I mean we must be follerin' somebody else. That ambulance Mellew was gittin' fitted out at Galveston had a fancy top bein' built on it. That wagon down there's jest a plain ole Dougherty wagon like the one Jakes and his partner is usin'. I musta slipped up somewhere."

"You can worry about it while we're looking for the ford. Now that Seymour Garnsey's on the Red I'm not much interested in finding your friend Mellew. Garnsey's all the trouble anybody needs. Let's make tracks."

Less than a mile above the wagon camp they saw what looked like a sand bar jutting out into the mud from the far shore. A fair sized creek emptied in at that point and its wash had evidently brought down a lighter sand than the usual river silt. This would provide the easiest crossing for miles, better than the one the peace party had used on the trip to the Washita. Even wagons might ford the river at this point without getting into the mud that blocked such a move at most points.

"We'll wait right here," Hale told the older man. "It's better than keeping an eye on the wagons. If there's to be any kind of move by those men on the north side this is where it'll have to be made."

"What was ye expectin' might happen?"

"I don't know. This could be a good spot for guns to disappear into the Nations. Once across the Red the trouble would be started. I don't want that to happen."

Tolliver changed the subject with suspicious haste. "Did ye git a good look at that big wagon back there, Cap'n? It wasn't like nothin' I ever seen out here before."

"It was big enough to hold a lot of guns," Hale said grimly.

"That oughta be the way of it. Sure as hell them ambulances ain't the Mellew wagon—neither of 'em. I wonder what he done with the one I was watchin'? And where is he now?"

"Keep wondering," Hale advised. "If you get yourself mixed up enough maybe you'll start telling me the whole truth about this. Meanwhile, I don't think I'll fret too much over Mellew; I've got Garnsey."

When the dig failed to draw further talk Hale said only what was needed in the business of setting up their position. He knew that Tolliver kept muttering to himself, but he let the old man do his own worrying. There was enough to think about without the useless wondering that mere curiosity could cause.

They made coffee in another foggy dawn, getting rid of their fire before a light westerly breeze could break up the river mists. It was going to be hot. Both men moved to a spot where they could look out at the sand bar, their horses safely picketed in light timber behind the ridge. Only minutes after the mists began to burn off they knew that some of their guesses had been pretty accurate. Riders were moving through the timber which fringed that creek beyond the ford.

It took a little time for the watchers to make out details, but then the distant horsemen moved into the open and Hale knew that he was studying one of the small outlaw bands which had made the Red River frontier so notorious. Two of the men now edging out to the sand bar were Indians. One was a Negro. The other pair, now riding ahead, were either white men or half-breeds of some sort.

"Nice combination," Hale grunted. "I wonder if this is part of the gunrunning deal or if it's just a gang of bandits looking for plunder?"

"Don't make much difference, does it?"

"Not to us. If there's guns in those wagons I'm out to make sure that they don't get across the river. It could be almost as bad to have extra guns getting into the hands of guerillas and outlaws as it would be to have them going to Indians. But let's play it careful. Maybe they're not the outlaws they look. Maybe none of this is what we think it is."

"Waitin' and lookin' suits me fine, Cap'n. There ain't no point in borrerin' trouble when a man mostly gits plenty of it give to him fer free."

Hale laughed quietly. "Is that a genuine Tolliver proverb or are you fixing to blame that one on Ben Franklin?"

Tolliver elected to ignore the thrust. With some dignity he suggested, "Better stick to lookin', Cap'n. Them polecats is movin' out into the ford. I reckon things is about to start happenin'."

The five men had moved slowly out to the point of the sand bar and had halted there in an apparent discussion of the narrow channel which looped around the end of the bar. They didn't seem to be in any hurry, merely curious rather than concerned about the easy crossing they were about to make.

"Mellew among 'em?" Hale asked.

"I dunno. I never seen Mellew. Didn't I tell ye that?"

"You told me a lot of things. I never know what to believe."

"They're comin' on across."

Hale studied the still-distant riders. Two of them were definitely Indians although they wore a combination of white man's clothing and buck-skins. The Negro and both white men were mostly in dusty blue like the outfit Hale was wearing. General Banks's clumsy operations along the lower valley of the Red had outfitted not only a lot of enterprising Confederates but also half of the outlaws in the region. Union supplies seemed to turn up everywhere.

"Lemme do most o' the lookin'," Tolliver hissed as he crawled forward through the low brush. "Seems like my eyesight's real sharp this mornin'—and there ain't more'n half as much o' me to git spotted by them varmints."

Hale nodded agreement but moved to a spot where he could see through the bushes without exposing any of his long length. He didn't expect to see anything about the strangers that would make him change his estimate of them, but he still wanted to keep them in sight.

"Any sign of the wagons yet?" he asked Tolliver. "You can see around the bend better than I can."

"They ain't showin' yet. Got any plans about what we're goin' to do about these bastards?"

"Likely we'll have to fight. But wait and see. No use picking a scrap when we're outnumbered."

"Mebbe we ain't gonna have no choice," Old Ben muttered. "Them varmints is comin' right up toward us. If'n our broncs start to make a noise we'll be in a fight whether we like it or not."

"Maybe we could throw a bluff. They don't know there's only two of us."

"Damned poor chances on that deal. These fellers know there's a hangman waitin' fer 'em somewhere. They ain't goin' to surrender. They shoot fust and do their listenin' later—if there happens to be any later."

"Quiet. They're stopping. Let's see what they do next."

That was when a high-pitched voice snapped an order from directly behind him. The voice was muffled enough so that the outlaws wouldn't hear it but there was still a sharp ring of menace in it.

"Don't make no noise, neither of yo'! And don't try to swing them guns around! Ah got yo' covehed."

Chapter 3

Hale rolled over cautiously until he could see the freckled snub-nosed countenance which showed between the brim of a disreputable hat and the top of a clump of bushes. Even then he could see only part of the face. That unwavering carbine hid most of it.

"Don't get careless, son," Hale advised, as calmly as he could manage with that big bore gun holding steady on him. "Nobody's looking for trouble."

"Not that yo' need go fur to find hit," the voice hissed, carbine still steady as a rock. "Trouble's raht down theah a piece." This time Hale thought that he could detect more of Tennessee than of Texas in the drawl. More important, he knew that the hushed tone was a recognition of the outlaw threat. This boy didn't have to be an enemy.

"Why throw down on us?" he asked mildly. "You say yourself that the danger's down below us."

"Ah couldn't trust nobuddy 'til Ah found out about a couple o' things. So talk fast! What's yore game, mistuh?"

"Put the gun down. We're Texas Rangers on special duty." It didn't seem like a bad idea to include Tolliver in the classification. Explanations were simpler that way.

"Rangehs?" The voice seemed to rise a note as

doubt came through. "Rangehs wearin' them Yankee blue shirts. An' that fancy hat?"

Hale managed an uneasy chuckle, hoping that the challenge had not been heard down the hill. "Everybody's got Yankee blue shirts nowadays, even the men who just came across the river. All but Sergeant Tolliver, that is. He's such an honest jasper that he don't like the idea of stealing supplies from the Feds." It seemed like a good idea to try for the lighter note while he was building up the impression about Ranger duty.

The carbine came down slowly. "Ah reckon Ah gotta trust somebuddy, bein' as how them polecats down the hill ain't up to no good. Better yo-all than them, seems like." The speaker rose as the carbine went down, giving both men a good look at the faded cotton shirt. The shirt told its own story.

It was Tolliver whose high voice became practically a squeak as he exclaimed, "Damned if'n it ain't a woman! What the hell!"

Hale certainly wasn't going to argue the point. This was a woman, all right. At least this was a well-matured girl. The round face, freckles, and short nose had suggested a boy but that impression definitely ended at the neck. The cotton shirt couldn't even begin to conceal an impressive roundness.

Her carbine had snapped back into position at Tolliver's exclamation and her voice became harsh as she ordered, "Don't try nothin', damn yo'! An ole goat like yoreself ain't got no call to be gittin' no smart idees!"

Hale broke in hurriedly, trying to get the girl settled down before she could betray their presence to the men on the lower slope. He sensed that her show of toughness was a cover for a fear she was too proud to show so he made a fresh effort to be calm and casual about the whole thing. "Easy. I take it you're just as concerned as we are about the men who just came across the river. What can you tell me about them? What do they want over here on this side?"

She stopped glaring at Ben and turned to eye Hale with calm speculation. "Ah know this much about 'em, mistuh, that they've been follerin' us on the otheh side o' the Red fer three-foah days now. Ah nevah seen more'n a couple of 'em at a time but now they got moah—and they ain't on the otheh side no longeh! They ain't up to no good!"

"You mean you're the one who's been doing the scouting for your wagons?"

"Yep. Ah'm a good scout. Ah sneaked up on yo' real good, didn't Ah?"

Hale grinned. "You've got the best of me there. How long have these men been watching your wagons?"

"Since jest about the same time them fust folks caught up with us. That'd be mebbe a week."

A few ideas had begun to sort themselves out in

Hale's mind. This girl wasn't the one who had made those woman tracks Tolliver had reported. Probably she had left the sign Hale himself had studied on the ridge.

"How many in your party?" he asked, taking a quick look at the gathering below. Nothing much was happening down there; maybe he could get a few things cleared up before any trouble could start.

"Three wagons—since yestidday, that is. Fust off it was jest me and Uncle Golly. Then them folks in the ambulance caught up with us and stuck along. That was a week ago—when Ah fust begun to see them polecats across the Red. Yestidday we picked up another pair. Two men in another ambulance. It makes six of us altogether."

"Where are your wagons now?" He thought he should ask the question even though he already knew the answer.

"Raht around that fust bend down-river." She pointed with the carbine. "They oughta be showin' up real sudden now. They was neah ready to move when Ah rode up the ridge. Ah was fixin' to ride back and warn 'em about them polecats when Ah seen yo-all. Ah had to git things figgahed out so Ah throwed down on yo'."

"I understand. Do you have time to ride back and warn them now?"

The girl shook her head. "Too late. They'll be showin' any seccont."

Tolliver passed a husky warning that the outlaws were picketing their ponies in some thick cover halfway up the ridge and a little to the left of where the three watchers were hidden. When Hale squirmed forward he could see the gang clearly enough. They were dismounted now, one of the white men obviously issuing orders and motioning toward the brush directly below the watchers.

"Looks like they're fixin' to set up a ambush right smack in front of us," Old Ben growled. "I take it we ain't gonna let 'em do it?"

By that time the girl had crawled down to take a position beside Hale. "Ah dunno about yo'-all," she whispered, "but Ah ain't fixin' to let 'em!"

"Take it easy," Hale soothed. "I'd like to know more about this. For a while I wondered if these men were coming across to meet some of your outfit, maybe because they had it all fixed to make a meeting here. Now it seems like we can throw that idea away. So tell me what they want. Is there anything in any of those wagons that would bring outlaws out of the Nations on a job like this?"

"Nothin' as Ah know of," she told him. "Uncle Golly's fitted up to git into the Injun tradin' business, bein' as how there ain't no business left in Texas, what with the blockade and all. He picked up some pore grade cotton stuff and some Mex leather. It don't seem like nothin' to stir up no raid."

"What about the others?"

"Ah dunno much about 'em. Them Mellews ain't haulin' no great grist o' stuff in their wagon and it didn't look to me like them other varmints was loaded real heavy. Ah dunno fer sure." As she spoke she began to wriggle forward into a better position for observation. The move was worth seeing. Ragged denim pants covered thighs that were as neatly constructed as the spectacular upper part of her body. It was easy to forget that her face wasn't on a par with the rest of the assembly.

She turned her head and caught Hale's stare. "Quit leerin', damn yo'!" she snapped, her voice still a whisper but with sting in it. "Ah know jest what yo're thinkin'. All yo' he-critters are jest alike!"

Hale grinned awkwardly, matching her whisper as the outlaws began to move across the slope in front of them. "So it's nothing personal. Keep your head down; they're coming this way."

Then he aimed another whisper at the grinning Tolliver. "Mellew's with the wagons. You heard what she said."

"It still ain't the right wagon."

They fell silent as the gang began to take positions pointed out by the blackbearded thug who seemed to be in command. The listeners could hear him plainly enough. There could no longer be any doubt about it; there was to be an ambush of the oncoming wagons.

Hale wondered why. He had a feeling that the girl had told the truth. These wagoners were not gunrunners. What did the outlaws want? Simple plunder?

He calculated the distances involved. Wagons following the narrowing flats along the mud would pass within some thirty yards of the ambush position. At that range the affair could turn out to be mighty bloody unless something could be done to stop it. For the moment he could forget Garnsey, the guns, even the lie Tolliver had certainly told. As a Ranger, even a temporary one, he had a clear duty to protect travelers against bandits.

The girl seemed to be reading some of his thoughts. "Yo're gonna lend a hand, ain't yo?"

"Of course. How did you plan to handle it before you found us? Were you going to tackle them singlehanded?"

"Don't git sarcastical! I'd ha' tried it if'n I couldn't see no other way."

"I believe you would. Let's move down a little. There's still good cover ahead. Maybe we can hear a bit more about what they plan to do."

She moved forward at once, wriggling through the low bushes and using the cover most efficiently. Hale exchanged grins with Old Ben and the pair of them followed. Going into battle behind such a well rounded pair of pants and that kind of a wiggle was going to be a bit of a novelty.

"Good thing I'm an ole man," Tolliver muttered . . . "if bein' ole kin have anything good about it."

The girl selected good cover and within moments all three of them were behind a screen of brush where they could look down directly on the outlaws. The blackbearded man was talking to the Negro and a smaller white man that he called Jed. One of the Indians, a squatty, bandy-legged fellow, had trotted down to the flats once more, evidently to watch for the wagons coming around the bend.

"How much of a fight will your people put up?" Hale asked in a whisper. "How many fighting men in the party?" He was still going on with the pretense that he knew nothing of the wagoners.

She didn't turn her head as she hissed a reply. "If'n they put up any fight at all Ah'll be plumb surprised. Uncle Golly ain't wuth a damn—and he ain't got no gun. Mellew could be better'n Ah give him credit fer bein', but don't depend on him. Them otheh apes ain't nothin'. Jest city folks."

Hale made no comment. He was listening to the sudden explosion of wrath from the blackbearded man.

"Ye're takin' my orders, Goddammit!" the man snarled. "We wipe 'em out! That's final!"

"But that woman could . . ."

"Shut up!" Blackbeard raised his voice a little, repeating orders for the benefit of the whole gang.

41

"Remember what I told ye—all of ye! We ain't leavin' none o' them bilge rats to do no talkin'. Shoot careful. Don't hit none o' the stock. No tellin' what we'll be needin' before we git clear."

Jed tried once more. "Ain't no call to kill Mellew's woman, Lorry. She'd make us a right nice pet back there in the hills. And she wouldn't slow us up none."

"Shut yer trap, I told ye!" The burly man was shouting now. "We got the jump on that damned double-crossin' Maddigan and I aim to keep it that way. I ain't takin' no chances jest so's ye kin have a woman. Not as ye'd know what to do with one nohow!"

When the little man tried to protest the big fellow roared again, still trying to impress his authority on the others. "Maddigan ain't gonna be long in findin' out that somethin' went wrong with his cute little scheme. The longer we keep him guessin' the safer our hides is gonna be. Jest keep thinkin' about that. We ain't takin' no chances on somebody ever doin' no talkin'!"

He waved the Indian sentry farther out into the open, repeating the orders he had evidently given earlier. The ambushers were to fire on his signal—and not before. The sentry was to kill the lanky man on the big wagon. The Negro would take Mellew. The smaller white man was to get the little man on the wagon that had joined up last and the other Indian was to aim at the extra new man. Lorry himself would be ready for the scout who usually rode the ridge above the wagon trace. It seemed clear that the outlaws did not know that the scout they had been seeing was a girl. And they did not name any of the company except Chris Mellew.

"Heard enough?" the girl whispered in Hale's ear. "It's cold-blooded murder they're plannin'. Let's git down there where we kin give 'em a dose o' their own medicine."

"We'll move down," Hale agreed. "Carefully. But we don't do any back-shooting. I'm a lawman and I've got to handle it my way. I'd like to catch some of this gang and find out what they're up to. Right now I think it's more than a plain old outlaw raid."

"Don't be a damned fool! That kind ain't gonna give up."

Hale knew that she was right. Men who took refuge in the Nations did not dare surrender. Still he had to make an effort. "We do it my way," he told her bluntly. "Get ready to obey orders or get out of here!"

When she didn't reply he went on, "Make up your mind, sis. Are you with us or not?"

She still didn't look around. "Ah suppose Ah got to do like yo' say—stupid as it is. And mah name ain't sis. It's Susie."

"Fair enough, Susie. Here's what I want you to do. The minute we see your wagons coming out

43

from behind those cottonwoods you're to start working your way across toward the spot where the gang left their horses. They'll be watching the wagons so I don't think there's much of a chance that you'll be spotted. I'm going to make a try at bluffing them into surrender. It probably won't work but I have to try it. Your job is to cut them off if they make a run for the horses. Ben and I will try to make sure that you don't get rushed by too many of 'em."

She turned to meet his glance then, a wry smile turning her urchin features into something almost cute. "Better not be more'n one of 'em headin' mah way," she murmured. "This heah cahbeen don't reload easy. Ah still think we oughta cut some of 'em down. It'd be healthier."

Hale showed her the Colt revolver he was carrying. "Brand new, with the good intentions and bad management of the Union army. It'll take care of the odds against us. Now get ready to move out."

"That Injun's makin' signals," Tolliver announced hoarsely. "Wagons must be comin'."

"Ah'll do it yore way," the girl whispered. "Jest keep in mind that Ah ain't goin' to git but one shot if'n it comes to a hurry-up fight."

"Don't go if you don't want to."

"Ah'm goin'. Don't let 'em git too thick on my part o' the hill."

By that time the squatty little Indian was trotting up the slope toward his hidden companions. The girl waited until he disappeared into a thicket and then she moved away, making perfect use of the cover available on the slope.

Old Ben murmured his appreciation of her skill. "Knows how to handle herself," he told Hale. "Mebbe in more ways than one."

"Keep your mind on your business—and hope she's good with her carbine."

"That part'll be fine. When she had the damned thing pointin' at us it didn't do nothin' but hold plumb steady. All her wigglin' seems to happen in more interestin' places."

They could see the big wagon beginning to show through the cottonwoods so it seemed that the travelers had not changed the order of march. Tolliver began to mutter again. "I can't figger out about them Injuns," he complained. "Never seen none what looked jest like 'em. Strange breed to me."

"Osages, I think," Hale whispered with some impatience. He had a feeling that Ben had mentioned the Indians to forestall any comment about Mellew or the woman who seemed to be with him. "What difference does it make? Renegades show up in every tribe, white, black, or red. Our job now is to make sure that none of the red ones get away. We can't have Indians, renegades or any other kind, showing up at those peace talks with a report of fighting here along the Red. It would ruin everything."

Four rawboned oxen emerged from the cotton-woods then, dragging behind them an immense, high-topped wagon. Hale thought of medicine shows he had seen touring the country before the war and he felt certain that this wagon had once been in that kind of business. It was big enough to contain sleeping quarters or to be converted into an open-air stage for whatever act went with the sales spiel. Its colors had faded pretty badly, probably because of the poor-quality paint available behind the Union blockade, but he could tell that a really gaudy job had recently been attempted. The girl's account began to sound truthful enough.

Then he studied the tall, white-bearded driver. That would be the Uncle Golly the girl had mentioned. A man like that on a wagon like that would have a name like that. And he might still be a gunrunner.

The other two wagons came into view behind the big one. They were almost identical ambulances, probably from that supply base Tolliver had mentioned. Wagons intended for Hood or Johnston might well have been bought cheaply— or stolen—after Union control of the Mississippi made it impossible to deliver them to Confederate forces in the field.

Chris Mellew looked much as Hale had pictured him from Old Ben's description. Tolliver hadn't actually seen the man—or so he claimed—but he had heard him described and had studied his tracks. As Ben had reported, the fellow was of medium stature, stocky in build, and of dark complexion. He was a little too well dressed for the frontier, but he was not quite as dandified as the pair on the third wagon.

The blackbearded man called a cautious order to his men. "Don't git careless. That's Chris Mellew on the second wagon but he ain't no more important than the others. We got to wipe 'em all out."

"But that there yaller-headed woman ain't . . ." Jed was still being persistent.

"Shut yer face! And don't think I ain't aimin' to git rid of her jest because she ain't one o' the fust targets. I want that scout fust, then I'll fix her!"

Hale was calculating distances as carefully as possible. He hadn't seen any rifles in the hands of the outlaws so he guessed that they would wait until their victims were at very close range. He had wanted to wait also but now he decided to make a move before the whiskery man could start looking for the missing wagon scout.

Without exposing himself he yelled suddenly, "Drop your guns! I'll kill the first man who tries to turn around. Quick now! Throw 'em down!"

There was an instant of flat silence but it was no more than the time he used in shouting. Then the desperadoes reacted as they were almost certain to do, perhaps guessing that the man behind them was the lone scout they had been watching. For them anything was a better bet than a surrender.

It was the Negro who made the first move. He jumped to his feet recklessly, trying to swing a musket around. The weapon never came to his shoulder as Tolliver's carbine slug knocked him backward down the hill. Suddenly Hale found himself with more enemies than he could handle, even with that fine new six-gun in his fist. The Negro's move had given the other outlaws the chance they needed.

Three of them were running hard toward their horses but the big man showed more fight. He twisted around and blasted off two quick shots with a revolver, one of the slugs cutting brush just above Hale's head. They were searching shots but they were much too close for the man to be ignored. Hale drew fine, knowing that he could afford neither time nor cartridges. Susie was going to need his help in a hurry.

He toppled his man with the first shot and turned the six-gun on a running Indian. This time he missed so he jumped to his feet, almost falling over Tolliver and knocking the ramrod out of the old man's hands.

Down along the river the wagoners were doing a lot of frantic yelling but Hale didn't look toward them. He had to hope that they wouldn't start firing until they knew the difference between friend and foe. For the moment he had to put all of his attention on helping the girl.

Ahead of him a carbine banged and a bullet clipped his sleeve. He went to one knee and blasted away at the young Osage who had halted to reload. This time he did not miss. The odds were better already.

He could hear Tolliver cursing a bent ramrod so he knew that he could expect no help from that quarter. Then another gun slammed and a man began to scream. The brushy slope kept Hale from knowing what had happened but he was sure that Susie was in plenty of trouble. At least two outlaws had reached the thicket where the ponies had been left—and the girl had only a single-shot weapon. He had to get to her as quickly as possible.

He wasn't quite fast enough. The firing ceased but he could hear a horse galloping away. Then he broke through a screen of bushes and saw that it was Jed who was making good his escape. There was no sound of movement on the hill but he moved with increased caution. It was no time to get stupid.

Chapter 4

For a moment or two there was silence on the brush-covered slope. Then Tolliver began to swear happily before yelling, "Where are ye, Cap'n? I got the damned thing fixed."

"Over here." Hale turned completely around, scanning the area as he replied. There had been two Indians in the gang. If either of them now lay wounded there would be danger. Young hellions like that would generally try to kill before giving in to their wounds.

Still nothing stirred. Hale yelled, "Take a look down the slope a bit. Be careful." He knew that the warning was not really needed but it seemed that he ought to issue it.

Then another voice broke in. From some bushes almost in front of where he stood he heard Susie drawl, "When it's clear, Cap'n, yo' might gimme a hand. Ah got that damned redskin but the otheh fella caught me while mah cahbeen was plumb empty."

Hale jumped toward the sound of her voice. Susie was flat on the ground behind a bush, her right hand across her breasts to hold hard at a reddening patch beneath her left armpit.

"Lie still," he ordered as she raised her head. "No point in trying to look brave. You're hit."

"Ah sorta guessed it," she told him dryly, only a slight trace of strain in her tone. "Somethin' shore hurts like hell where it hadn't oughta." The pallor beneath her tan told him that she wasn't feeling as chipper as she was trying to sound.

He took a quick look at the Indian sprawled on a ledge several yards below them. The warrior was obviously dead, a bloody patch covering his entire chest. That big-bore carbine of Susie's had made quite a hole.

The girl caught his glance and spoke again. "Ah hit him good, hey? Did the otheh polecat git away?"

"Yes. Too many of them for you to handle alone. It's my fault. Now let's see how much of a wound you're carrying."

"Jest a scratch, Ah reckon. Leastways Ah could still move around before Ah got to feelin' a mite giddy."

"Don't try to move now. Let me take a look and we'll see what we need to do about getting you patched up."

She gave him a crooked smile as he pulled the shirt tail loose and began to slide it up above the area where her hand was pressing. Since she wore nothing under the shirt it quickly became apparent that his earlier estimate of her physical attractions had not been in error.

"Keep yore mind on the hurt," she half whispered, letting her bloody hand drop away so that he could push the shirttail up above the wound. It seemed to him that she was almost enjoying herself, probably because she knew that he was embarrassed.

He used the bloody garment to wipe away the smear, seeing that the bullet had torn a rather nasty gouge across the fleshy part of her side just beneath the armpit. He didn't think that the ribs had been touched but she was going to have a mighty sore side for a while. The important thing now was to halt the bleeding.

"Messy but not real bad," he told her cheerfully. "Got a clean bandana or anything like that?"

"Hell! Who kin keep anything clean in this dusty dam' country? Jest wad up the shirt and use it. There ain't nothin' else."

He nodded agreement, rolling the shirt so that it made a pad beneath her arm. "Easy to hold it there by keeping your elbow close to your body," he told her. "Stay put and I'll get a horse. We'll fix you up a bit more comfortable when we get you down to the wagon."

"One thing," she called to him as he started away. "Yo'll do the fixin', won't yo'?"

He turned to stare in surprise. "Why should I?"

"There's some Ah don't want foolin' around."

"You've got a woman in the crowd. What's wrong with having her do it?"

"Me'n her don't git along."

Hale couldn't quite understand what he saw in

the girl's dark eyes, so he swung away impatiently. "You'll have to get along with her on this!" he snapped. "I'll see to it!" He didn't know why he had to feel so grumpy about the matter. The chore would certainly have its interesting features.

The yelling continued while he went for horses. Tolliver had started to reply to the questions the wagoners had been howling ever since the firing ceased so the danger of panic shooting seemed to be over. The wagon people still didn't know what had almost happened to them but they knew that they were no longer in any particular danger.

Old Ben came across as Hale reached the horses. The younger man gave swift orders. "Look after everything, Ben. See if you can find anything to identify the dead white man. And keep an eye on the outlaws' broncs. In case we didn't see all of the gang we don't want trouble over an attempt to grab the horses. Find out everything you can about this mess."

"Girl git hit?" Ben asked.

"Flesh wound. I'll get her back to her wagon."

"Right." The old man's grin hinted that he was holding back some sort of comment about the happy features of such a chore.

Hale found Susie on her feet, drawn face pale but her expression indicating that she intended to keep control of herself. "Hang on to your hurt," he told her. "I'll boost you into the saddle. We'll look for your horse later."

"Ah kin git up mahself," she retorted coldly. "Ah don't take help from them as ain't willin'."

"Stop sounding like a woman. This time I help. Down at the wagons somebody else does it."

"Ah'll sound like a woman if'n Ah want to! Ah got a right to!"

"I noticed. Now stop squawking and let's get this job done. I got you into this mess—at least partly—so I'll take care of you until somebody else can take over. Then I've got work to do. One of those bandits got away."

"Ah don't need yo'!"

He didn't argue but simply picked her up and set her on Tolliver's horse. She made quite a nice armful even if she didn't smell like the women he had held in more polite society.

She handled the horse without help after that, easing down the slope toward where the wagons waited with their occupants standing around in a show of tense excitement. The four men Hale had already seen from a distance and the fifth person in view was a woman who was just about as different from Susie as she could be. Dressed much too fancy for the frontier trails, she wore her yellow hair piled elaborately on her head to glint in the warm May sunshine. Hale estimated that she might be in her middle thirties, her height making the roundness of her figure seem in nice proportion. She seemed to be reasonably pretty but as the distance shortened he saw that her prettiness had a

54

haggard quality about it. This was the woman the outlaws had referred to as Mellew's woman, the one Ben had identified by her tracks at the camp site. Oddly enough, the thought that crossed Hale's mind then was that he should remember the mistake Tolliver had made in not reporting two women with the wagons. The next time the old man began to brag about his sign-reading prowess this mistake could be brought up as a squelcher.

He pushed the half-humorous idea aside as something else became more important to him. He had seen this blonde woman before. He even knew her name. More important than that, perhaps, he knew quite a lot about her.

At that moment Susie seemed to think that her escort needed information about the people ahead. "That's my Uncle Golly holdin' the ox team," she said in a low voice. "The tall lanky old man with the white whiskers and the big feet. Mellew's standin' there by our wagon and the woman on the seat of the second wagon is supposed to be his wife. Which Ah doubt. Them last two jiggers calls theirselves Garnsey—which is the little one—and Jakes. They jest showed up a day or so ago." The words trailed off a little at the end as though the effort had been too much for her.

Hale eased his horse closer so as to be in a position to grab for her if she started to fall. "Thanks for the fill-in. Now stop talking and save your strength. I'll take care of everything."

She looked up quickly. "Yo' mean yo're gonna . . ."

"No. I mean I'll see to it that the woman does it. Don't be so damned edgy about her. She'll handle the chore real good."

Then he had to start answering the questions that were being fired at him by the anxious wagoners. "Outlaw gang tried to ambush your party," he shouted for all of them to hear. "Your scout helped break it up. Forget the details and lend a hand. This girl saved your hides; somebody see about patching up a hole in hers."

Susie was heading toward the big wagon and Hale let her go. She had control of herself now and seemed to want to be on her own. It gave him a chance for a good look at the stocky, dark-faced Mellew. The man seemed to think that the glance was an invitation for him to take charge for he promptly demanded, "Who the hell are you and how come you're bustin' in here takin' charge o' things?"

"Tom Hale. Captain. Texas Rangers." That part came out crisply enough and he followed it with something just a little more crisp. "I'm taking charge because that's my job. Don't go out of your way to get snotty to somebody who just kept you from getting massacred."

"We'll get you a medal," Mellew sneered.

Hale turned away, seeing that the white whiskered man had moved out to help Susie from the saddle. When the big man was on the ground it was easy to appreciate how tall he really was. Even the big feet didn't look so big when they were part of all that length.

"Are you Uncle Golly?" he asked as he slid from the saddle to help brace the girl.

"Yep."

"Can you take care of her alone for a few minutes? I'll get that woman over here to do the bandaging."

Mellew had followed by that time and Hale got an even closer look at the man, noting that the swarthy complexion was really a deep tan. Mellew was in his early forties, his skin weathered and with deep wrinkles angling down from the sides of his nose to the corners of his mouth. The lines seemed particularly deep as the man growled, "You're bein' damned high-handed around here, Mister Ranger Captain. We'll take care of our own without you movin' in to give orders."

"Don't be a damned fool," Hale told him calmly. "Just get that woman of yours over here. The girl needs help."

For a moment it seemed that Mellew might try to make an issue of the suggestion but then he apparently decided that he wasn't on very strong grounds. "Get her yerself!" he snapped. "It ain't no skin off'n my butt." Then he turned and strode away.

"Kinda touchy," Hale said, frowning. "I wonder what's itchin' him?"

"Me," the girl told him briefly. "Forget it. Let's git this bleedin' stopped. I'm gittin' to be a mess."

"Sorry," Hale said. He strode quickly across toward where the blonde woman maintained her position on the seat of the second wagon. She seemed to know what he wanted for she greeted him in a tone that was almost as offensive as the one Mellew had used.

"I won't lay a hand on that dirty . . ."

Hale's interruption was harsh even though the words could reach no ears except the pair directly in front of him. "Think twice before you refuse, Betsy!"

"My name is Belle Mellew!" The harshness in her tone didn't quite cover the panic. "*Mrs.* Belle Mellew."

"Don't make me drag this out into the open. I don't give a damn whether you're now Mrs. Belle Mellew or not. When you knifed that Yank lieutenant in New Orleans you used the name of Betsy Appleby. And it wasn't Mrs. anything. The reward posters call you a camp follower—with due charity."

"You're a liar!"

"Don't be stupid. Come over and see what you can do for the girl. It'll be better than to have me start talking."

"You can't blackmail me, you sonofabitch!" She was shrill but her voice was still little more than a whisper. "We're not behind the Union lines."

"But you're keeping your voice down. You're afraid Mellew won't like it if he finds out that you hornswoggled him into hauling a wanted murderess around the country—and letting her pose as his wife."

"You're lying!"

"You know better. Likely you also know that your hide might be just a bit in danger if Mellew found out. He's the kind who might just turn you in for a thousand dollars reward money. That's the amount as I remember."

Her tone changed swiftly as feet crunched on the dry gravel behind Hale. "I'll be happy to help out with the unfortunate creature," she said loftily. "Where will I find the proper medical supplies?"

Hale grinned knowingly. "Thank you, Mrs. Mellew," he said with great formality. "I appreciate it but I'm not able to help much. You will have to ask someone else about supplies." Then he winked at the blonde and warned, "Better have plenty of bandages; you've got a lot of scenery to cover."

He turned, face straight now, to meet Mellew's scowl. The swarthy man said nothing, however, and Hale went back to where the old man was getting things ready for his patient. Susie was still standing erect, pressing the left elbow at her side to keep the makeshift pad in place and fanning herself with the ragged wide-brimmed hat. Hale noted that her hair was close-cropped and much the same shade of brown as his own except that the sun had put an auburn tinge in it.

The thought was a brief one, crowded out by a number of other things demanding attention. There was the almost completely exposed breast and the trickle of blood which now was soaking into the waistband of Susie's pants. There was a quick memory that one or more of these wagons might be loaded with stolen muskets intended for renegade Indians. It wasn't easy to concentrate on anything.

He went to the girl, steadying her with one arm while he watched the tall old man attending to some hooks and catches at the side of the big wagon. Uncle Golly was letting down a sort of trapdoor that disclosed a sleeping compartment, whose raised cover served as a sort of outside awning when it was open.

At the same time Hale got a good look at the wagon itself. He guessed that the clumsy looking vehicle had once been painted red but that a mass of lettering had subsequently been added. Most of the work had been carefully but not very professionally done, colors having been the big thing in the mind of the painter. Across the broad side of the wagon "GOLIGHTLY SHATTUCK" had been painted in big yellow capitals that must have been brilliant before the Texas sun went to work on them. A second line was made up of smaller letters, but the lack of size was offset by the use of multiple colors. It had required blue, green, yellow and a sort of sickly orange to spell out "ALL KINDS OF TRADE GOODS." The trapdoor which Mr. Shattuck had just opened carried the words—in blue—"NAME IT AND WE'VE GOT IT." A smaller trapdoor at the front, actually under the side of the driver's seat, had green letters that spelled out "BEST DEAL IN THE COUNTRY." By contrast with all this color Mr. Golightly Shattuck was alarmingly dull in his bib overalls. The patches were faded out even worse than the girl's outfit—and without those redeeming features.

Betsy arrived then with crisp orders for Shattuck. She wanted bandage material, whiskey, and any kind of drugs his traveling store might carry. She listened to his report that he carried a good healing ointment and plenty of whiskey and that he could tear up cotton goods for dressings. Then she swung to face Hale, expressionless as she ordered, "Help me lift her into that damned bunk. One good thing about it; I won't have to stoop over to work on her."

They picked Susie up between them and raised her into the cubicle. She had started to protest at the move but then she sagged and the color went out of her face.

"Get that whiskey," Betsy snapped. "Then both of you go 'way and let me alone. Your room's more valuable than your help."

Hale nodded, making sure that he got a good look into the big wagon while Shattuck was getting the supplies out. The vehicle was pretty well loaded but there was no sign of any boxes of the right size to contain firearms. Not muskets, at any rate. Probably Susie had told the truth.

As he went back to his horse the two men who had remained with the third wagon came across to meet him. It was Garnsey who took the lead, his air of importance hinting that he proposed to make himself heard. Hale didn't want to wrangle with the man but he didn't propose to be patronized by him either. The Garnseys of the South had already caused more than enough trouble for the Tom Hales.

"See here, Ranger," Garnsey called when he realized that Hale was about to get back into the saddle without waiting for him. "I want a word with you. I think it's about time you made some kind of report."

Hale made himself keep his voice low. "Report?" he echoed. "Nobody around here to report to."

The little man seemed about to explode. "See here, Captain! I hold credentials as the lawful representative of the Governor of Texas. I demand a report from you!"

Hale swung into the saddle, using the move to help him restrain his anger. When he turned to look down at Garnsey there was actually a grin on the powder-stained whiskers. "Demand and be damned," he invited casually. "Now get out of the way before I ride you down!" It seemed to him that he had waited a long time to enjoy such a moment so he put plenty of fire into the order. It was about time that somebody threw a scare into the Garnseys.

When the little man jumped hastily behind a wagon Hale turned to yell at Mellew. "You, Mellew! Get a horse and ride up on the ridge with me. I want you to see if you can identify a bandit."

The stocky man started to snarl a protest but Hale cut him off as sharply as he had silenced Garnsey. "Stop arguing! That gang of cut-throats named you. They were ready to kill the rest of this crowd just to make sure that they got you. I want to know why. Come along!"

He didn't even look back. He had had his moment of blowing off steam and he felt better even if it had been a bit childish. Now he had to get on with business. Searching for hidden guns could wait. The first in his order of business would be an attempt to find out what this attack had meant.

Chapter 5

He tried to think things out as he set his horse to the climb. So much had happened in such a rush that there had been no time to guess what it meant. For the moment all he knew was that outlaws had been out to get a man named Mellew, a man Old Ben claimed was running stolen guns to the Indians. The trouble with accepting the obvious explanation was that Mellew wasn't using the wagon Tolliver had described and there were certainly no guns in the one that had been under attack. Hale had gotten a good look while he argued with Betsy. This ambulance didn't contain much of anything.

When he was well above the bottomland he looked back and saw that Mellew and Jakes were following him, both astride horses they had not bothered to saddle. It made him wonder about Jakes. Ben claimed that the lean man had been watching that mysterious wagon at Galveston— and now he was out here. Who was he and what was he doing with Seymour Garnsey?

A carbine shot sounded then and Hale looked hastily to his own weapon, feeling more than a little guilty that he had not reloaded after the fight. It was the kind of mistake an experienced man should not have made, even when things had been so mixed up. Maybe he wasn't getting back into harness as quickly as he had felt he was.

"All right up there?" he shouted.

Tolliver's high voice came back promptly. "Jest makin' sure about this red polecat. Did ye git the gal down the hill all right?"

By that time he could see the little man examining a broken musket. "The girl will be all right," he called back. "Did you find out anything about the gang?"

"Nope. What about yerself? Git any idees about why them wagons is all headed up the Red?"

"Not much. One way or another it's not gunrunning, I'm sure. We'll take more of a look later."

"Any of 'em say what they was aimin' to do?"

By that time Hale was close to the old man. "I didn't do much asking. First things first. Right now I've got Mellew coming up here to take a look at the whiskery gent. We'll see how he acts. I told him that the man mentioned his name."

"That wasn't too shrewd, Cap'n. Now he ain't gonna be surprised."

Hale shrugged. "I slipped up in other places, I'm afraid. So far I just keep getting confused. Maybe because I've been listening to too many lies."

Tolliver used his old trick of changing the subject. "I picked up a good gun from that bandit," he announced, holding up a revolver which looked a lot like the one Hale carried. "It ain't a Colt and I can't make out no name."

"Foreign copy, likely. The man was shooting mighty good with it. Find any ammunition? Could be a different bore."

"I got what he had in his pockets—which wasn't much. Mebbe there'll be more in a saddlebag. I ain't had no look at the hosses yet. Didn't seem like they'd be carryin' no more identification papers than the men was." He cackled happily at his own humor and added, "That's a kind of a joke, Cap'n. Git it?"

Hale shook his head wearily. "Bad quotes are all I can stand, Ben. Don't start making bad jokes. Anyway, it won't keep me from believing that you still haven't told me the truth about this mess. Where's the whiskery gent?"

"Right where ye cut him down. He ain't been real spry lately."

Hale turned to wave directions at Mellew and Jakes. Then he rode across to where the outlaw leader had fallen. Sight of the dead man seemed to bring out a couple of half-conscious ideas that he hadn't found time to consider. Mellew was no frontiersman but he carried a heavy tan and the seamy skin of a man who had been much exposed to weather. Something in his speech and manner had suggested the sea—and the outlaw chief had used the term "bilge-rat." Maybe there was a connection.

66

Mellew and Jakes arrived on the scene then, Mellew grunting a little after the bareback ride. The sailor idea looked better all the time.

"What the hell's the idea of all this?" the stocky man growled. "Maybe you're a Ranger and maybe you ain't. One way or another it don't give you no call to git so damned bossy!"

"Don't start that again! I've got a job to do— even if I don't know exactly what it is yet. I propose to do it, with or without your help. Now, take a look at this dead man and tell me who he is!"

Mellew's glance had already strayed toward the corpse and Hale had not missed the quick start of recognition. Now, however, the stocky man was ready. He simply shook his head. "Never seen him before in my life."

"You're sure?"

"Damn it, mister, I . . ."

"Stop shouting. I think you're lying but let's try it another way. Does the name Maddigan mean anything to you?"

"No." The denial was prompt, maybe a little too prompt. Then the man recovered some of his poise and asked in a milder tone, "Is that the name of this dead man? I mean, *was* it?"

A smart question, Hale thought. It was the kind of question that an innocent man might have asked. He decided to see how far Mellew would try to play the role. "Maybe I ought to tell you what I know," he said quietly. "We spotted this gang across the river and guessed that they would be bad ones. This morning we watched them make the crossing so we holed up to watch some more. About that time the girl—your scout—showed up and told us about your wagons. The gang set up an ambush just below us and we could hear them talking."

"Did they say what they wanted?" Mellew asked quickly.

"Just that they were on the trail of a man named Mellew. Somebody else—this Maddigan jasper—also seems to be on your trail and our black-bearded friend ordered the whole wagon outfit killed off so there wouldn't be anybody left to tell Maddigan what had happened to Mellew. The little man who got away—named Jed, by the way—wanted to capture the blonde woman but the boss man wouldn't agree to it. Blackbeard seemed to be named Lorry or something like that. Does any of it make sense to you?"

He had watched carefully as he supplied details but there was no real reaction. Mellew simply hunched his heavy shoulders and said, "Means nothin' to me. I don't know any o' them names."

"What have you got in the wagon that they might want?"

"Not a damned thing. Only some trade goods that I figured would get me through the Indian Nations. I'm headed for Santa Fe."

"Why?"

"It's none of your damned business, but I don't want to be in Texas when the Yanks take over. That's enough for you to know."

"How many was in the outlaw gang?" Jakes interrupted. He also had been watching Mellew with some intensity.

"Five. Jed got away, shooting Susie when he made good his escape. We killed a couple of renegade Osages and a Negro. And Lorry, of course."

"I just wondered. Sounds like just another band of outlaws."

"That's how I figured it at first. Then they mentioned Mellew and I changed my mind."

"Then change it again!" the stocky man growled. "I don't know how anybody got my name into it."

Hale kept the same casual tone. "Sergeant Tolliver is taking a look at the outlaws' ponies. Want to see if he found anything?"

"No," Mellew retorted. "I'm not interested."

Jakes grinned and announced, "I'll go along, Captain. I'm curious."

Hale led the way around a shoulder of the ridge, walking his horse and watching to see whether Mellew would follow. The stocky man hesitated only a moment and then rode straight back toward the waiting wagons.

There was no further talk until they closed in on

69

the spot where the outlaw ponies were tethered. Then Jakes asked abruptly, "Had any late word from Headley Stiles, Captain?"

Hale swung around slowly, meeting the thin man's direct gaze. "Who's Headley Stiles?" he inquired.

Jakes grinned again, showing a couple of gold teeth. "I don't blame you for being careful but we'd better understand each other. I happen to know Stiles pretty well. I know that he got a Ranger commission for you because you were the only man he trusted to look after that peace commission on their trip to the Washita. I also know that the pair of you are making plans to get into the cattle-drive business when this war finally gets finished. You could use this job because it gives you a good chance to take a look at Indian country and to decide whether there might be a better trail than the one Oliver Loving worked out back in fifty-seven."

Hale continued to stare. "Did you ride up here with me to tell me how much you know about me?"

"In a way. It's the only way to make you understand that the rest of what I want to say is worth hearing. Stiles tells me that you're to be trusted. After the way you snapped at Garnsey I think I know what he means."

"I wish I knew what *you* mean."

"Patience, Captain. I'm getting to it. You already

70

know how much most Texans are depending on this peace conference. We know that the Confederacy is done. Some time this summer—if it hasn't happened already—there will be an end to the fighting. Then we have the problem of untangling the mess. We have to get back to business before we starve. We've got the Yanks to worry about and we can't afford any extra worries over Indians. Whether a deal is made by the Confederacy or not we've got to have peace on this frontier!"

"That part's clear enough. Future cattle drives are not the only businesses that will depend on it. Any kind of Indian trouble might set us back for years, not to mention the killing that would be involved."

"And that's where my job comes in. You know Garnsey, I take it?"

"I know he was one of the hell-fire secessionists who got us into this mess. I wouldn't put it past him to be trying some scheme to stir up more trouble."

"That's exactly what he seems to be doing. The diehards want to turn the peace talks into a deal with the Indians. Texas is to supply arms and ammunition for the redskins to start a series of attacks on Union settlements. Garnsey tried to get himself included in the peace party so he could work for some such scheme but Stiles kept him out of it. Now the old bastard's making a try on his own."

Hale did not admit that he had already heard rumors. All he asked was, "Is the man crazy?"

"In a way I suppose he is. Anybody with a grain of sense has known since Vicksburg that the war was lost. Our best bet was to make peace while we could hope for easy terms—but idiots like Garnsey wouldn't let us. They've caused a lot of needless killing and we're at the point where all we can do is take what the Union gives us. If word gets around that we're trying to turn savages loose on the western towns we'll get a brand of military occupation that'll be worse than war itself."

Hale nodded his agreement. So far Jakes sounded all right. The man was stating the sentiments of men like Headley Stiles, men who had tried to keep their heads when good sense seemed to have gone completely out of style. "What's your part in all this?" he asked.

"My job is to stop Garnsey. Stiles sent me to investigate when the first rumors began to circulate. Garnsey and his outfit didn't know me. Nobody does. That's part of my stock-in-trade. On this chore I'm Albert Jakes. I've used other names and they don't mean any more than this one does. Anyway, I managed to make good old Seymour believe that I was just the man he needed as an aide and pretty soon I found myself heading for the Washita with him. He still hasn't told me what his plans are but at least I know what to suspect."

"But what do you think he's trying to do? Even

a Seymour Garnsey can't believe that he'll start an Indian war by making political speeches to the red brethren."

"You mean you didn't get word about those stolen muskets?"

"No details. And Garnsey wasn't mentioned."

Tolliver broke in quickly. "Mr. Stiles didn't tell me no more'n I told ye, Cap'n."

Hale waved him to silence. "He didn't mention it in his letter. That's what I'm talking about."

"He didn't know," Jakes explained. "They were keeping it quiet, trying to find out what happened. When I left Stiles all he knew was that there were rumors. I was to see if I could track them down—with Garnsey as chief suspect. Then I got wind of two hundred Harpers Ferry muskets missing from a depot outside of Galveston. It took a while before I could get anybody around there to admit it and by that time Garnsey was ready to move. I came along with him."

"Then you don't know whether he's got a hand in the gunrunning?"

"No, but I'd bet on it. He's too damned smug. I've played cagey but he won't bite at any of the bait I've dared to throw out. I'm sure he's up to something, but I don't know what it is."

"What do you know about Mellew—and Lorry and Jed and Maddigan?"

"Not a thing. They may be mixed up in it but I don't know anything about them."

"How do you plan to stop Garnsey if it does turn out that he's trying to arm the tribes?"

The thin shoulders came up in a shrug. "Murder, likely enough. He's got it coming to him. Captain, you've been on the Washita. You know how tough it's going to be to make any kind of treaty with the Kiowas, Arapahoes, Southern Cheyennes and the rest of them all mixed up together and anxious to look big in front of each other. They're a lot more likely to listen to war talk than they are to peace talk, particularly when the Cheyennes have been on the warpath for more than a year already. Garnsey and guns could set off a blaze that would sweep the whole Southwest. Anybody's crazy who'll believe that Indians can be turned loose on Colorado settle-ments and not start raiding Texans as well."

He broke off suddenly, swinging his horse to ride back. "I'd better join the others," he said. "No point in having anybody wonder why I'm spending so much time up here with you."

Hale watched him in silence until he disappeared over a hump in the slope. Then he aimed a quizzical glance at Tolliver. "What do you think, Ben? By the way, you're Sergeant Tolliver to these people. We may be able to handle things a mite easier if they think we're both official."

Old Ben chuckled, but shook his head. "I can't figger that jigger. Most o' what he said sounded

74

all right but he was lyin' when he claimed he didn't know nothin' about Mellew. I tell ye I seen him hangin' around that wagon at Galveston. It wasn't no big secret about the wagon and who was havin' it built."

"Don't you think it's about time you told me the truth about that part? I've got enough troubles as it is without wondering what's back of your talk about wagons."

"Ye mean ye ain't tumbled yet? Didn't them names mean nothin' to ye?"

"What names?"

"Maddigan. Lorry. Even Mellew."

"I never heard of them before."

"Ever hear of a boat called the P. Nellie P.?"

Hale stared impatiently. "Dammit, Ben, if you've got something to tell—the truth, I mean—get on with it!"

"Take it easy, Cap'n. Ye know the old sayin' about a watched pot not gatherin' no moss. Mebbe it wasn't Franklin what said it but . . ."

"Get to the point!"

Old Ben looked pained. "Well, Cap'n, it musta been about the time ye was gittin' back from N'Awlins so mebbe ye didn't hear about it. This here blockade runner, the P. Nellie P., started out to make a run fer Jamaica but didn't hardly git clear o' the passes when a Yank gunboat put a cannon ball right into her waterline. She got clear o' the Yank but sunk in shaller water at night."

"The Penelope," Hale broke in. "I heard the story—or part of it."

"That's what I said. The P. Nellie P. Anyhow, she was haulin' a cargo that mebbe ye didn't hear about."

"So tell me."

"Gold. And mebbe some jewelry. Seems like there was plenty o' folks what had been makin' a good thing outa blockade runnin'—even if'n they didn't let on to nobody that they was pilin' up the loot. When they got to smellin' an end to the war they tried to fix it so's they wouldn't lose none o' their profits. The skipper of the—whatever her name was—was haulin' out valuables that the smart folks didn't want to have around fer the Yanks to find. Mostly it was hard money, the yarn claimed. Anyhow, there was stuff on the ship what nobody was supposed to know about 'ceptin' the skipper."

Hale nodded. Some of the story sounded familiar even though he had paid little attention to it when he had heard it. Fresh out of a Union prison-camp hospital he had found little interest in anything of the sort. Perhaps the tale had even added to the bitterness he felt against people who'd made a good thing out of the useless killing of other men.

"Nobody seemed to have the straight of it," Ben went on. "The ship went down right inside one o' them passes, but it was thick fog and nobody on shore knowed what was goin' on. The skipper disappeared. Mebbe he was murdered by the crew or mebbe he drowned. There was both kind o' talk. Mellew was a kind of second mate what had been ship's carpenter before men got so scarce that they had to promote him. One yarn had it that he was the one what helped the skipper hide the stuff aboard the boat in the first place. Anyhow, this here Mellew was missin' fer a week after the wreck and folks figgered he drowned with the cap'n—or run off with him. Then Mellew showed up with a tale about bein' alone on one o' them little sand bar islands and not bein' able to git off. Nobody could tell different."

"But you think he was mixed up with some bit of plundering?"

"Seemed like there might be a damned good chance of it."

"How does it mix in with this gunrunning story?"

"I dunno, Cap'n. I didn't . . ."

Hale's voice was low but bitter as he interrupted, "You never even heard about the guns until Stiles told you! Getting me onto Mellew's trail was just a trick! Damn you, Ben, you could be shot for a trick like that! Stopping that gun shipment could be just about the most important thing that'll happen in Texas for the next few years—and you get me off on the trail of some imaginary plunder! I should . . ."

"Hold up a bit, Cap'n," Ben pleaded. "I ain't told it all yet. That wagon at Galveston. I was watchin' it—along with some other fellers what wasn't no more'n curious about why a man would build a big top on a Dougherty wagon. Mellew give out that he was fittin' it up fer the Injun trade but the talk had it that he was goin' to smuggle his gold west. Anyhow, I loafed around there with the others and I seen quite a few folks come and go what wasn't jest loafers like the rest of 'em. Jakes was one."

"Not Maddigan or anybody else that we've been hearing about?"

"Nope. But them names popped up plenty often. Them sailors from the P. Nellie P. turned out to be hell-raisers after they was wrecked and out of a job. The supply base near there was guarded by a lot o' ole men and young sprouts. Them sailors robbed the place whenever they wanted somethin' they could sell fer licker money. The biggest bandit in the gang was the bos'n o' the ship, a big ape named Mad Maddigan. I ain't sayin' he stole that batch o' guns. It happened after Mr. Stiles called me up to Austin. But there wasn't nobody what knowed more about the supply base and how to raid it than this here Maddigan."

"And you know who Lorry was?" Hale had dropped his anger at this new bit of information.

"Yep. He was gunner off'n the P. Nellie P.

I figger him and Maddigan are chasin' Mellew because they think Mellew run off with that loot. I'm also bettin' that somehow they're mixed up with them guns. It fits real good."

"You mean it fits your purpose real good! If I believe that you haven't thrown me too far off the trail of the important part of this job maybe I won't try to beat you over the head."

Tolliver grinned. "Ye wouldn't do that, Cap'n. Mebbe I didn't work this jest the way Mr. Stiles woulda done, but I got ye plumb up against this here Garnsey polecat. No matter who stole them guns it's got to be Garnsey's game."

Hale surrendered. "I think you're right—and I can't understand how you do it. Your lies always turn out to be . . . Aw, forget it!"

Chapter 6

Hale turned his horse and ordered, "Let's get those extra broncs down to the river. Ours and the outlaws' both. And Susie's. We've got to get on the trail of that Jed rascal."

"Why? He ain't totin' no gold or no guns."

"I want to see where he goes. If he's wounded we might even catch up with him and make him talk. While we're chasing him I don't want this little collection of dubious characters to break up. Maybe it'll tie 'em up a bit if we leave them some extra stock to handle."

He had decided that temporarily he would have to accept Tolliver's new story at face value. It fitted with everything else that he had been hearing so probably it was as accurate as the old man could make it.

"What about havin' them wagoners take care o' these dead jiggers?" Ben inquired. "That'll give 'em somethin' to do. If'n they're gonna stick around here fer any length o' time they don't want to be smellin' corpses. Not in this hot weather."

"You're in charge," Hale told him promptly. "Sergeant Tolliver, send out a burial detail. Tell them to sink the corpses in the soft mud and make sure that they're covered. No need to dig."

Tolliver grinned. It was clear that he was much

relieved to have his lie exposed without more recriminations being aimed at him. "Now ye're soundin' like ole times, Cap'n."

"Forget it! In the old days we never had to handle anything nearly as big as this. Close to ten thousand assorted savages on the Washita and somebody tries to stir 'em up and take 'em guns! Let's get moving!"

They drove the extra horses before them toward the wagons, Hale adding one final bit of instruction. "Don't mention the Penelope unless somebody else does. We don't know anything about Ryan or Maddigan. We don't suspect Mellew. Just keep quiet. Let somebody else make the mistakes."

"What about Jakes? He seemed to have it purty straight?"

"I think he's all right for the most part—but he lied about knowing the Mellew story. Likely enough it's just another case of somebody letting themselves get turned from their duty by a gold yarn. If you know what I mean."

"I git the point. So we don't risk anything on Jakes neither."

"Right. I think he'll help keep the others tied up while we take a look at Jed's trail. It's a risk to hold them here with that Maddigan threat in the air but it's also necessary. I don't think Susie is going to be in any shape to move for at least two or three days."

Tolliver grinned. He was getting over his scare now that Hale didn't seem to be too angry. "Don't start talkin' about what kind o' shape Susie's in, Cap'n. I got eyes."

"Better use them to a different purpose—at your age!"

The whiskery grin didn't fade. "Ben Franklin said it, seems like. 'A man ain't old as long as he looks.' I ain't doin' no more'n lookin' but . . ."

"Stop babbling! Start acting like an efficient sergeant of Rangers."

The wagons were still waiting, teams still in harness. Nobody seemed to know what ought to be done next. That suited Hale. If they were waiting for orders they would certainly get some.

"One other thing you ought to know, Ben," he said quietly as they rode down the last pitch of the ridge. "That woman with Mellew. She's using the name Belle Mellew and claiming to be his wife. Actually she's out of a New Orleans bawdy house. Not one of the regular ones but one that was set up after Ben Butler took command and let camp-followers flood the city. Not that it makes any difference to us. The point is that she stabbed a Yank lieutenant and got away with a murder tag on her. The name she was using then was Betsy Appleby."

"I'll be damned. Things git real messy, don't they. Ye think she's in on the gold deal?"

"Forget the gold! It's guns we're trying to run down!"

They closed in on the wagons then and Hale called out briskly, "A couple of you men give Sergeant Tolliver a hand with these horses, please." He tried to make himself sound official and polite at the same time, hoping that he could avoid any kind of challenge from Mellew or Garnsey. "We'd like to get started on the trail of that outlaw who escaped."

Making it clear that he was leaving things to Tolliver he spurred across to the big wagon and dismounted. Betsy Appleby had already disappeared and Shattuck was standing awkwardly beside the compartment where Susie lay quietly with her eyes shut.

The lanky man laid a finger against bearded lips, whispering hoarsely as Hale came in beside him. "Job's done. Purty good, too, but that woman was awful freehanded with the whiskey."

Hale ducked low enough to look in under the trapdoor awning. He saw that a shoddy blanket covered the girl to the chin. The pallor behind her tan made her skin look ghastly but he thought the stage was beginning to pass. Perhaps the liquor had done it but something was bringing back a shade of proper color.

Suddenly she opened her eyes to stare up at him. "Real nice o' yo' to come back," she murmured. "An' Ah ain't meanin' to be sour-soundin'."

"How do you feel?"

She giggled softly. "Ah reckon Ah'm a mite drunk. Ain't feelin' no pain."

"Did Bet . . . Mrs. Mellew do a good job?"

In answer she used her right arm to sweep back the blanket and show him an ingenious bit of criss-cross bandaging which held the compress firmly in place. Anchoring strips passed alternately above and below the smooth round breast to give a straining effect that was almost startling.

Shattuck swore angrily. "Cover them things up, ye huzzy! I knowed ye got more licker in yer gut than on yer hurt!" He didn't wait for his order to be obeyed but pushed past Hale to yank the blanket back into place. "Dunno what Ah'm gonna do about her," he growled. "She gits more uppity all the time!"

Hale tried to smooth matters over. "Good job of bandaging," he said quietly. "The big idea now is to stay quiet. You'll have a bleeding problem if you don't."

"That woman had oughta sewed it up," Shattuck growled.

"No time—and likely she couldn't handle that kind of thing. Just keep the girl quiet. You'll have some time right here because I'm going out to see if I can find out where this Maddigan gang is. While I'm gone I don't want these wagons to move. You can help keep the others quiet for a while by reminding them that Susie shouldn't be jolted. Just unspan your oxen and make camp. It's not a bad place for it; the water's fairly close to this bank."

"I ain't got nothin' to do with them others," Shattuck told him. "I can't keep 'em waitin'. We jest happened to meet up along the river."

"That's all right. They'll get orders about staying here. I won't be gone long."

He had been trying hard to keep his voice casual. He wanted it to be that way when he spoke to the others. It wasn't going to be easy to shut out the thought of what a full scale Indian war might mean, particularly when he faced the man who was deliberately setting it up, but he didn't want to betray his knowledge of the facts just yet.

Mellew was objecting strenuously about the halt and Hale put forth a little extra effort to be impersonal as he approached the group. "Don't argue with the sergeant, gents," he broke in briskly but with a show of easy humor. "He's got his orders—and I've got mine. We're here to keep this trail up the Red and across to the Washita as peaceful as possible. We don't want anything busting up the peace talks, not even outlaw raiders. I'm asking all of you to stay right where you are until we can scout the country and see what's going on."

"Why the hell should we stick around and get murdered?" Mellew demanded. "Maybe we could get ahead of the trouble."

Hale fixed him with a stern glance. "Do you happen to know anything about that country over there, Mister?" His sweeping gesture indicated the land north of the river.

"Not a hell of a lot. It's Injun country but most of the Injuns ain't home now. They're up on the Washita."

"Most of them are. About ten thousand altogether. They were listening to peace talks when I left but they didn't seem much impressed. They're thinking about how the white men have been killing each other off for the past four years and they're listening to the Cheyennes tell about what easy picking they've been finding along the Platte. Any little thing could set them off. I don't want that little thing to happen here."

"If we keep goin' it won't."

"That's where you could be wrong. Restless Indians are not the only trouble-makers on the other side of the river. The tribes haven't used this part of the Nations much since the outlaws, guerillas, deserters, and runaway slaves started moving in. From the Red to the Arbuckle Mountains it's practically an outlaw state, the only Indians in the area are renegades like the pair we killed this morning. I'm guessing that this man Maddigan we heard mentioned is the leader of an outlaw band. He's supposed to be hunting for Mellew and he must be pretty close or that other crowd wouldn't have been so scared that he'd move in on 'em.

Mellew, you're the one who's bringing the danger; I don't think you've got any call to argue."

"Let him move on," Garnsey suggested. "The rest of us can stay here."

Hale silenced the angry exchange which ensued. "All of you stay!" he snapped. "I'm responsible for this stretch of country. I want you all together until I know what my job is going to be. That's an order so don't make me get tough about it!"

"We'll do as you say, Captain," Jakes put in. "What do you hope to learn by chasing this outlaw?"

"Anything will help. Maybe we could catch him and make him talk. Or maybe he'll try to join Maddigan now that his regular gang is done. Mostly I want to know which direction he's heading. It could mean something."

Tolliver had moved away to saddle spare horses and now he was coming back with the mounts. "I told 'em about shovin' the dead jiggers under the mud, Cap'n. Anything else?"

"That's all. I think they'll know enough to water the stock and keep an eye out for trouble. Let's ride."

They rode away silently, picking up Jed's trail without trouble. The fleeing outlaw had galloped straight up the river, evidently concerned only with putting plenty of distance between himself and the mysterious enemies that had ruined the outlaw plans.

"Looks like he didn't know what he wanted to do," Old Ben commented when the trail began to zigzag between the river and the tapering end of the ridge.

"Maybe afraid to venture into that open country ahead. I'd guess that he wanted to get back across the river and didn't dare cut back toward the ford."

Then they saw where the man had made his decision. He had sent his horse straight out across the mudflats. It couldn't have been an easy crossing. They could see marks of desperate wallowing in several places on both sides of the narrow channel but apparently the man had made it.

"Back to the ford," Hale said shortly. "Too bad we couldn't have outguessed the move. We could have gained quite a bit."

The return to the ford gave them a chance to see that the wagoners had settled down as ordered. Mellew and Jakes were watering the stock and Betsy seemed to have taken over the cooking chore. There was an exchange of waves but the distance was too great for any words to be traded. Hale simply tried to indicate by motions that they were hoping to pick up a trail on the north side of the river. It didn't matter very much whether they understood or not.

"Dam' funny about them people," Tolliver grunted when they were riding across the sand bar. "Mellew mostly. I ain't one to swaller treasure tales but it seemed like this 'un might be all to the good. With him fixin' up a wagon it looked real neat. A couple of his shipmates bein' on his trail makes it look even better. Now he's out here without the wagon—and no sign that the outfit he's usin' is more'n it looks to be."

"Forget the gold."

"Mebbe we hadn't oughta. Gold and guns could be all tangled up."

Hale nodded in spite of himself. "I've been thinking about it. Let's suppose Mellew brought the gold ashore and hid it. Other crewmen of the Penelope suspected. He makes a lot of false moves to hide his real trail—like fitting up a wagon he didn't intend to use. Meanwhile Maddigan gets into this gun-stealing game and he's on his way into the Nations with the guns. Somebody gets word to him that the Mellew operation still looks like live business. So Maddigan plans to catch Mellew, not knowing that Lorry Ryan is already trying it."

"Sounds possible. If'n Jakes gits gold hungry when he's on a chore fer Stiles there ain't no reason to think Maddigan couldn't git hisself switched over to the same deal. Gold's got a powerful hold on folks' imaginations."

"Like your own, for example."

"I ain't denyin' it."

"No use making wild guesses. Maybe we could beat some of the truth out of Jed. I think he might have decided to cut back after he crossed the river so we'll head straight north. With a little luck we might cut his trail and save ourselves time and distance."

"Figgers real good if he's headed fer outlaw country."

"So keep your eyes open. This grass won't leave a good trail and we can't afford to miss anything."

They had struck lush prairie almost as soon as they left the river. Sign wouldn't be easy to read, but a rider would certainly leave enough of a trail for them to spot it.

The strategy didn't work out. They were a good two miles north of the Red when Hale called it off. "Wrong guess," he said shortly. "Nothing to do but to head for the river again." There was no thought that sign had been missed. There wasn't an Indian in the Nations who could read sign any better than Old Ben.

"Too bad," Tolliver grumbled. "I'd shore ha' enjoyed tryin' to wallop some o' the truth outa that bastard."

Hale chuckled. "Now you know how I feel about you sometimes. Let's angle southwest and see what happens."

Ten minutes later it happened. They found a trail that was old enough to be blurred in the thick grass but it was still readable enough. Two wagons had gone through, accompanied by several riders and with a number of extra ponies behind the wagons. They had been headed for the river, their course almost parallel to the one Hale and Tolliver were riding. Old Ben's report didn't change Hale's snap judgment. This had to be Maddigan and the stolen muskets.

"Six riders," Tolliver reported after close scrutiny of the sign. "Figger a man on each wagon and it makes eight o' the bastards. Ye think it's Maddigan and them guns?"

"I think it's exactly that. How long ago did they pass here?"

"Two days, mebbe three. I ain't gonna git too cocky after the way I missed out on that other lot o' sign."

"No matter. If Maddigan was ahead of Ryan the chances are that he's up the river somewhere, likely enough with his own ambush set up. If Jed joins up with him he'll know what happened. Our people could be in trouble."

"What about the guns?"

"Maybe we're all in trouble."

Chapter 7

They followed the wagon tracks in silence for perhaps ten minutes. Then Tolliver pointed to the ground and announced, "Jed."

Hale could read the story easily enough. Bits of drying red mud on the grass identified the man who had cut the wagon sign at this point and had studied it for some time before following it.

"Plenty clear," Hale said when Tolliver moved as though to get out of the saddle. "Let's keep going. We could find out more than we expected."

"We ain't fur behind the polecat now," Old Ben stated. "The mud ain't dry on the grass. Could be we'll ketch him before he gits up enough nerve to try j'inin' 'em."

They rode with extra caution, moving from one bit of cover to the next as they neared the river. The trail was plain enough. Jed was hitting a fast pace but the wagon sign showed no evidence that the party in front had been in any particular hurry.

When they struck high ground which let them see the river they dismounted and led their horses, still keeping to every bit of cover available. Now the wagon track was a little more complicated.

Evidently the party had adopted pretty careful tactics on this stretch. Several times they had halted the wagons while riders fanned out as though scouting the river.

Then the trail split. Six horsemen, followed by Jed, had gone straight out across the mud. Jed's tracks looked only slightly fresher than the others so it seemed as though the mud consistency hadn't changed much. The important part was that the wagons had made no attempt to cross but had turned upstream, keeping to high ground above the bottomland.

"Now we've got a problem," Hale muttered. "Do we chase the wagons or try to figure out what that gang is doing on the far shore?"

"Smoke up-river a piece," Tolliver told him. "Mebbe a mile."

"So we follow the wagon sign. The worst we can do is to get a better look at what that smoke means." He didn't like the new development at all. If those wagons contained the stolen muskets—as he felt certain they did—they were now headed toward the Washita trail. Should he try to overtake them and destroy the weapons or should he make some effort to defend the wagon party he had left behind? It wasn't an easy decision to make.

Tolliver suddenly began to cackle. "That pore damned Jed," he exclaimed. "Near got hisself killed this mornin'. Then he wallered across that mud twice. Now he's got to git close to Maddigan's gang without stoppin' a bullet. Some days a man don't have much luck."

"My heart's bleeding for him," Hale growled. "Let's move. Now we've got to watch the cover mighty careful. Can't afford to be spotted from the other side of the Red or from this side."

Still they made good time along the ridge that flanked the stream. In short order they were directly across from the smoke they had been watching, moving into positions where they could study the opposite shore once they were sure that the wagons had not halted in the vicinity. They could see that there was a camp on the south bank. It was in open country but the distance was too great for them to identify any of the tiny figures around the fire. Neither of them spoke until a flurry of distant action developed. They could see two men riding into camp from the east, one of them well in front of the other.

Tolliver murmured softly as though thinking aloud. "They set up camp in the open so's they wouldn't git surprised by nobody. Mebbe expectin' Ryan and his gang to show up. They've had a sentry downstream and it looks like he's picked up our ole pal Jed. Leastways the feller in front is about the right size."

"But why are they camped over there—and with the wagons on this side? It's the wagons I'm worried about."

They watched in silence, each knowing that the

other would be interpreting the scene in the obvious manner. Jed was being herded toward the fire and then questioned at some length, mostly by a man who loomed almost twice as big as any of the others. After that it appeared that Jed was getting pretty rough treatment. Apparently the Maddigan gang was trying to slam him around a bit to make sure that he wasn't lying to them.

"Lucky for you I don't work that way," Hale remarked after the little outlaw had been knocked flat for the third time. "Jed gets slugged for telling the truth—because they don't believe him. You lie all the time, and I know you're lying, but nothing happens to you. There's no justice."

"Ye got it all wrong, Cap'n," Ben told him cheerfully. "It ain't the lyin' what gits a man into trouble. It's the doubtin'. Ye don't never doubt but what I'm lyin', so ye don't need to git mean about it."

"Maybe I should change my tactics."

Tolliver changed the subject abruptly. "Did ye notice them guns over there, Cap'n?"

"Don't tell me your eyes are so good that you can tell what kind of guns they're carrying!"

"That ain't the idee. Look close and ye kin see that them jiggers standin' around have all got long guns o' some kind. Either muskets or rifles. The feller what hauled Jed in was carryin' one. It ain't the kind o' hardware most saddle men use."

"You're right. I suppose they'd arm themselves

out of the stolen lot. Not much doubt about what's in those wagons."

"Then we chase the wagons?"

"No. I think we can take a risk there. Maddigan must have some good reason for splitting his gang and leaving the wagons over on this side. Maybe it's the hope that he can catch Mellew and the gold—if it exists—or maybe he's supposed to meet Garnsey somewhere along here and get paid for hauling the guns. One way or another he went to a lot of trouble to cross the river. I'm guessing that he sent the wagons to some hiding place while he makes a move of some sort."

"Sounds good—but what does it mean to us?"

"It means that we go back to our fine collection of new friends. I think the next move is going to involve them. I'd rather be in on it—for a number of reasons."

"Like Susie?"

"Maybe. I was the one who let her get into a spot where she got hurt. I guess I owe her something for that."

"That ain't what I meant."

"I know. Get your horse."

They rode back downstream in silence, Hale trying to figure out what action he ought to take. It didn't seem right to be riding directly away from that load of stolen weapons, but he didn't want to commit himself to any move until he knew a little more. Maybe he could beat something out of

Mellew or Garnsey. In a nice polite way, of course. That was one trouble about being a lawman.

The wry thought left him in a mood to be reasonably pleasant when Tolliver broke in with an obvious attempt to get his mind off the dilemma that faced him. The little man was elaborately casual about it when he remarked, "One thing about all this, Cap'n, ye're shore gittin' a chance to look at a lot o' country. Oughta soon figger out which way's the best fer a cattle drive."

"Stop trying to be so confounded cheerful. I had my mind made up on the cattle trail three weeks ago. It's best to stay west. River crossings are too much of a problem when you swing too far to the east."

"Seems like. Better to cross a lot o' little cricks than one big river, even if the big one's mostly mud."

Hale chuckled. "Sounds like one of your notorious quotations. Or are you just leading up to one?"

"Shucks, Cap'n. Why does it have to be either way?"

"Because I know you. When you get that innocent tone in your voice you're all set to spring Holy Writ or Ben Franklin on me—or what you claim to be one or the other. It's like your lying; I expect it."

"Hell! Ye make me sound like . . . I dunno what." Old Ben was trying to appear aggrieved, but his voice gave him away. He was delighted that he had interrupted Hale's worries for a few moments at least.

Hale decided to go along with it. "This time I think I know the saying you were getting ready to spring on me. Something about all of the rivers running into the sea but never stopping the tide from getting low. Right?"

"That ain't no proper sayin'—and ye know it. There ain't no sea on this deal. It's little cricks runnin' into big rivers."

"How about this one?" Hale persisted, letting himself relax. "Little drops of water, little grains of sand, make a lot of mud. You could easily blame that on Ben Franklin."

They were still bickering happily when they reached the ford and could see the wagon camp on the far bank. There was a brief alarm before the watchers identified them and Hale wondered briefly what various members of the party were thinking. At least one man wouldn't be too pleased at the information that was coming in.

He told them what the scouting trip had disclosed, offering no theories about the wagons. The point he stressed was that Jed had joined a gang that would probably be Maddigan's outfit.

"We know they want Mellew," he told them. "That means they'll try to hit us as soon as they've checked on Jed's story. We've got to get ready."

"Why should we get mixed up in it?" Garnsey

demanded angrily. "None of the rest of us ought to be in danger because of one man."

"I'll agree on that," Hale said quietly. "I think Mellew owes it to the rest of us to tell the truth about why he's the target."

"I don't know, dammit!" the stocky man stormed.

"Maybe we could find out if we searched your wagon. We heard enough to believe that it's not a personal grudge involved. And they didn't want your . . . wife. So it must be something you're hauling."

Mellew surprised him then. "If you want to search the damned wagon go right ahead," he snarled. "I'll tell you exactly what you're gonna find in it but you might as well look. Then maybe you'll be satisfied!"

Hale promptly dismounted and left the horse standing. "Get on with the job, Sergeant," he told Tolliver. "You know how to handle this sort of thing."

He turned as though to ask something of Betsy but the blonde woman shook her head. "No use askin' me about it. Nothin' in there o' mine that he can bother. I ain't got nothin'."

It suited Hale's purpose to pretend that he had no great interest in the search so he walked across to the Shattuck wagon where Susie was watching developments with keen interest.

"How's the patient?" he asked. "Pain easing up any?"

"Ah hurt all over," she told him, trying to smile. "Even mah haid. That trade licker Uncle Golly carries shore ain't fer me!"

Betsy had followed him to the wagon, carrying a bottle with her. "I brought some brandy. Mellew will holler but let him. Maybe she could ease herself off with some o' this and not get hit as hard as what that other stuff did to her."

"Lemme alone," Susie protested. "Ah don't need it. Ah ain't gonna make no fuss about a bit o' pain."

"No good in talkin' to her," Shattuck interrupted from behind Betsy. "She's plain obstinate when she's feelin' good. She'll be wuss now."

"Ah ain't obstinate!" she flared. "It's jest that yo' always make out like Ah ain't got sense enough to be more'n a two-year ole!"

Hale turned away quickly. It seemed pretty clear that the rancor between Susie and her uncle was a matter of the old man trying to keep her a child even though she must be at least twenty and capable of doing a man's work on scout duty. He could understand the girl's angry resentment, but he didn't want to get mixed up in anything of that sort. There was trouble enough without tangling in family quarrels.

He had taken only a dozen steps when he found Betsy at his side. She took his arm as she pulled even with him, her voice low when she asked, "Could I have a quick word with you?"

He halted at once. "About your patient?"

100

"No. About me. I'm scared."

"Any particular kind of scare?"

"The part about somebody following Mellew. It looks like I joined up with the wrong man. What did I get myself into, Captain?"

"I'm not sure yet. Maybe you can help. How come you're with him?"

"It seemed like a good idea at the time. I was . . . well, you know enough about me so I might as well give you the whole story. I got through the Union lines after I stuck a knife in that pig and . . . believe me, Captain, he was awful! I'm no prissy young thing, you know, but he . . ."

"Get on with the rest of it. Are you working up to telling me what Tolliver's going to find in that wagon?"

"Oh, no. There's nothing to find, I'm sure."

"Very well. How did you get through the Union lines?"

Her smile was a little grim. "You could say I worked my way through. A patrol coming out at night. Anyhow, I made it. Then I found myself in some Godforsaken little town in east Texas and Mellew was there. He persuaded me that I shouldn't head for Galveston but should go to Santa Fe with him. I didn't mind. It seemed like a good idea for me to put plenty of distance between myself and New Orleans. Lots of other scared folks were talkin' of movin' out before the Yanks could take over so I didn't think Mellew was different from the others 'ceptin' that he was gettin' started."

"How did he say he planned to make Santa Fe?"

"Like he told it to you today. Trade with Indians along the trail. It sounded all right to me but now I'm thinkin' I might as well ha' let the Provost catch me as to get murdered along the trail out here."

"What kind of trade goods is he carrying?"

"Junk. Just plain junk." She seemed to be putting a lot of emphasis into the statement.

Tolliver picked that moment to back her up. He hopped out of the ambulance with his usual agility, howling his report at Hale. "Ain't nothin' in here wuth a damn, Cap'n. Cheap jools fer the Injuns, some fair to middlin' skinnin' knives—and some patched Yankee uniforms what look like they mighta been stole off dead men after a battle. Nothin' fer bandits to want."

"See?" Betsy whispered. "That's what scares me. I don't see why anybody would want to chase him but that's what they're doin'!"

"We'll find out," he assured her, not quite knowing what he meant by it. Maybe he was just speaking his own hopes.

He left her and went across to where Tolliver and Mellew were exchanging a few acid remarks. He broke in at once. "Seems like we can forget any ideas about Mellew carrying valuables—but it doesn't alter the fact that he's the one subject to attack. Tonight we'll post a sentry at all times and see if we can find out what that new gang plans to do. Any objections?"

"What difference would it make if we objected?" Garnsey snapped. "You seem to be running things in a mighty high-handed manner. Suppose we should decide to move on immediately?"

Hale grinned at the cockiness of the little man even though the mere sight of Seymour Garnsey brought back the old bitterness. Garnsey and his fellow secessionists had preached hatred of Yankees until they'd made people overlook the fundamental foolishness of secession. They had used emotional outbursts to spur enlistments. The Garnseys did the talking; other Texans could die as a result. The entire Ranger force had been mustered in to Confederate service as Terry's Texas Rangers. The Garnseys had proclaimed it as a proud record. The Rangers had suffered seventy-five percent casualties.

"I'll make it an order," Hale told the little man, his voice hard, the grin fading. "Tonight you take a turn on guard duty. The others I ask. You I order. If you want to get nasty I'm just the man you're looking for!"

He shook off something Jakes seemed to be on the point of saying and went on quickly, "Let's figure out a defense—always assuming that we have to beat off an attack. What weapons are available?"

The answers were not happy ones. The only gun in the Shattuck wagon was the single-shot carbine

Susie had carried. Garnsey had no weapon at all. Jakes had a pair of single-shot pistols in his luggage, both of them clumsy dragoon pistols of Mexican War vintage. Mellew had a Harpers Ferry musket of the same type that had been stolen from the warehouse at Galveston. Hale wondered briefly if this weapon had once been part of the lot that now filled those two wagons up the river a few miles. Likely not. Harpers Ferry muskets were nothing but old model Springfields. Both armies had used plenty of them ever since the beginning of the war.

He checked with Tolliver on the weapons they had picked up after the morning fight. Ryan's revolver was the only one worth counting. The only decent carbine had gotten its lock broken when its owner fell. Ben had found extra ammunition for the six-gun when he searched the outlaw's saddlebags, but that was the only good part of the report.

"Get everything ready," Hale told them shortly. "We'll set up guard shifts later. Right now I want to keep an eye on the upper river. As soon as they start believing Jed they'll begin sending out scouts. I want to be ready."

There was another idea in his mind as he rode up toward the flat area above the ford. He couldn't be certain that he was doing the smart thing in letting any delay take place. Those two wagons on the north bank might even now be rolling straight toward some concentration of renegade Indians.

Chapter 8

The hasty reconnaissance didn't tell Hale very much but it gave him a chance to be alone and to do some thinking. He saw no sign of an outlaw sentry, but just before he turned back he caught sight of smoke against the sunset. That was the way he had hoped it would be. Maddigan and his gang would be doing some figuring on their own. They didn't know whether to believe Jed or not. Jed couldn't tell them much about the force that had hit the ambushers. Before they could make a fresh move they needed more information. Hale guessed that he could count on delay while they were getting it. The wagons would certainly not make any important move while Maddigan was tied up with this other business, whatever it might be.

He felt reasonably optimistic when he rode back to camp, even though he knew that there was no reason for such optimism. Everything was a matter of guesswork. He wasn't sure that it was Maddigan up the river. He wasn't sure that the two wagons contained the stolen guns. He didn't know why anybody was on Mellew's trail. He didn't know . . . there didn't seem to be any good in dwelling on the thought. All he could do was to get ready.

He made his report sound cheerful enough when he returned to the wagons. "No change," he told them, explaining how he thought they would have acted after Jed's report. "I don't even think they'll make a move tonight—but we'll still keep sentries posted."

"Then they've got the trail blocked?" Shattuck asked.

"Yes. But maybe it's better that way. If they plan to attack us—and I assume that they do—I'd rather have them in front where we know about them than somewhere in the rear without us having any hint that they're there."

"Now you sound like an idiot!" Garnsey sheered. "Getting pleased over having murderers waiting for you!"

Hale grinned at the others. At least he hoped that something cheerful would come through the crop of whiskers. "Mr. Garnsey's nervous," he noted. "First time he's had to move toward trouble. Always he talked somebody else into going out where the bullets were flying. This is different."

"Captain, you're impertinent—and insubordinate!"

Hale kept the grin. "And in charge," he added. "So don't start talking about insubordination. You might draw a dirtier chore than I was fixing to give you."

He shut off the little man's protests and got on with the business of setting up watches for the night. "One man on duty at all times. Short shifts for two reasons. I want our sentinels to stay put, not to walk up and down on the skyline army style. That's a good way to get shot. Because you'll be keeping down and quiet you'll get sleepy in a hurry. So we change guard once an hour."

Susie's voice came from her bunk. "Ah'll be corpril o' the guard," she announced. "Ah been sleepin' all afternoon so it ain't likely Ah'll sleep much tonight."

"You'll stay right there in your bunk!" he retorted firmly. "Anyway, we'll need somebody who can move around good to wake up the relief men."

"Ah could holler."

"A great help that would be! Might as well have everybody stay up all night as to have 'em hearing you holler every hour. I think we'll make Mr. Garnsey the corporal of the guard. He probably wouldn't be safe to trust on a regular post and anyway all he ever did was to put other people on duty. We'll let him stay awake and change guards. If he falls asleep, Susie, you can wake him up. That'll wake up everybody else and they'll know who to blame for the disturbance."

Garnsey was fuming, almost too angry to get the words out. "Captain, I'll make you suffer for this insult! I know how little your commission means! I'll . . ."

"You'll never get home to protest if you don't shut your mouth. Start taking orders for a change! You may have to take worse if I find what I think I'm going to find in those wagons up the river!"

He left them to think about that remark, walking across to take a look at the captured horses while supper was getting finished. He remembered that he still hadn't taken any real look into two of the wagons he proposed to defend. It was pretty clear that neither could contain any kind of weapons like muskets but he still realized that he should make a search. Tomorrow would be soon enough.

The night passed without incident, Hale and Tolliver doubling on the more critical morning watches. Susie did not have to do any yelling. Seymour Garnsey appeared to be rather thoroughly cowed.

It was beginning to break day when Hale saw that someone was coming out from the wagon camp as though to join him at his post on the ridge. At first he thought he was seeing Ben Tolliver in some kind of unexpected move but then he saw that the figure was much too stocky. He let his hand drop to his gun butt as he shifted his position. It didn't seem like a smart move to trust Chris Mellew very far.

The man seemed to guess what was in his mind. "No hostile intentions, Cap'n," he called out when he was within easy earshot. "I wanted to have a talk with you when them other folks ain't breathin' down my neck."

"You mean you've decided to stop lying about yourself?"

Mellew laughed. "You're callin' the shot, Cap'n. I didn't figure you'd be fooled for long. So now I'll start over." He seemed curiously cheerful at the way things were working out. "I lied because it seemed like I had to. Now it looks like I made a mistake. That was Lorry Ryan what tried to ambush us yesterday. The big man up the river has got to be Mad Maddigan. You said you found wagon tracks and that fits out just right. Maddigan's the man what stole them guns outa the warehouse at Galveston."

Hale tried to hide his amazement at this frank statement. "Mind telling me why those men were out to get you?"

"I'm comin' to it. Ever hear of a ship called the Penelope?"

"I heard the name." He was still trying to keep his astonishment under control. He wasn't sure what he had expected of Mellew but certainly it hadn't been anything like this. "There was some talk about the Penelope when I was a prisoner of the Yanks. Sunk, wasn't she?"

"Yep. I was her second mate. We tried to slip outa one of the passes in a fog, headed for Jamaica. Sudden like we popped outa the fog bank straight onto the guns of a Yank blockader. We took a couple o' real bad hits before we could get back into the fog bank. By that time she was settlin' fast." He went on with the story almost as Tolliver had told it, dwelling a little more on the period he had spent alone on a barren stretch of sand just off the mainland.

"The point is that she was haulin' some valuable stuff. I never found out what the stuff was but there was talk of it bein' money and jewels. The skipper was takin' it out for folks who didn't think the Confederacy could last much longer."

"But you never saw it?"

"Hell! I never even heard about it 'til I got off that sand bar and found out how folks was gossipin'. They even claimed that I killed the skipper and hid the gold! Ryan and Maddigan thought that way. They tried all kinds o' ways to trap me with this stuff I was supposed to have. All they managed to do was get into each other's way."

"How come they thought it was you who had it?"

"I ain't sure. Yarns git started sometimes and you can't figure out how. Anyway, I decided to get clear of the coast country before the Yanks could move in. If a Yank officer got to believin' the kind of tale that was goin' around he could make it mighty nasty for me. It seemed like a good idea to go some place else."

"What about Ryan and Maddigan?"

"They both kinda dropped outa sight, almost like they decided they was ready to believe I didn't have what they thought I had. Then I heard about this gun warehouse bein' robbed. Scuttlebutt said it was Maddigan runnin' the show. It sounded like him. He'd go for a job that'd pay off good and get him outa east Texas."

"Then you knew that the guns were to be brought out here?"

"That was the way the story went. Guns for some kind of Indian fuss old Garnsey wanted to stir up. I think you got onto that in time, Cap'n. My guess is that Maddigan's along the Red because this is where he's to deliver the guns and get paid."

"Now you're making it sound confused," Hale protested, still trying to estimate the amount of honesty in the man before him. "If Maddigan is only here to meet Garnsey how does it happen that Lorry Ryan thought you were the main target?"

Mellew shrugged. "Maybe Ryan didn't know. Gold's a funny thing, Cap'n. It makes men do crazy things. Lorry musta figured that I had this Penelope loot so he picked up some outlaws for a gang and got on my trail. Then he heard about Maddigan bein' out this way so he guessed that Mad was on the same chore. Maybe he was right and maybe he wasn't."

"Then you don't have any way of knowing what Maddigan wants?"

"Only guessing, like I just told you."

"And you're not carrying gold?"

Mellew laughed. "You know better'n that, Cap'n. Your man searched my wagon real good. Have him do it again, if you like. I ain't got a thing that a greedy feller like Mad Maddigan would want."

"The danger's just as great," Hale pointed out. "Ryan was ready to do wholesale murder—not because you *had* anything but because he *thought* you had it. Maddigan could be the same way."

"That's partly the reason I thought I'd better tell you the whole story. You're a lawman; maybe you can get Maddigan to listen to reason."

It was Hale's turn to utter a scornful laugh. "What makes you think he'd listen to me? A man running guns to Indians don't get into happy little conversations with Texas Rangers."

"Anyway, now you know how it figures. I'm the poison, all right, but I dunno what I can do about it now."

Hale was puzzled. It didn't seem likely that the stocky man would have changed his attitude so completely, even if fear had begun to gnaw at him. There didn't seem to be any course but to go along with the new story and see how things worked out. At least there seemed to be good reason to think that those guesses about the musket shipment had been fairly accurate. What could be done about the problem was not so simple.

By that time Tolliver was coming up the ridge with a horse for Hale. That had been the understanding between them when Hale took over the sentry post. If nothing happened during the night they would make a daylight scout up the river.

"Tell the others to sit tight and wait for us to have a good look at things," Hale told Mellew. "Get breakfast over and water the stock. Be ready for a quick move if we need to make one."

The scouting trip proved barren. There was no sign of anyone moving in the area where the outlaw camp had been spotted, no tracks to show that any scout had come down-river during the night. It left Hale with an uneasy feeling that he might be permitting those guns to get away from him.

"What did that Mellew polecat want to talk about this mornin'?" Ben asked after a while.

Hale told him. "The story matched pretty well with yours. I don't know how to explain the differences in the part about the gold but that's neither here nor there. What I've got to think about is the part about the guns. Somehow we've got to take a hand."

"And it ain't gonna be easy. Too damned many of 'em—even if we could forgit all about these other wagon folks. Which I reckon we can't."

"Not yet, anyway. Are you sure there's nothing hidden in Mellew's wagon?"

"Damned sure, Cap'n. He's got racks built in to

hold his boxes o' trade goods. I hauled every one of 'em out and looked underneath. There ain't no gold there."

They went back to the wagons without further talk, finding the usual coffee, bacon, and biscuits waiting for them. This time the fare seemed to be better than it had been before and Betsy joked about it, claiming that she was finally learning how to cook. Her manner hinted that she was joking to cover her worries and Hale could understand it. There was plenty to worry about.

None of the others tried to match her humor. A night of broken sleep had left them edgy, openly irritable. The two men ate in silence, watching Jakes and Mellew taking the animals to water in small groups. Garnsey was snoring under his wagon.

After finishing his rough meal Hale went across to ask Susie, "How'd you get through the night?"

"Purty good. Mostly nobody bothered me. That Garnsey polecat didn't need no stirrin'."

"See anything out of the way?"

"Like what?"

"I don't know. All I'm thinking is that I don't know who to trust in this crowd. Likely they've all done a bit of lying and I'd like to figure out some of the truth. I thought maybe you could help."

"Meanin' that yo' trust me more'n the others?"

"Why not?"

"Thanks Ah didn't figger yo' liked me very much."

"That's got nothing to do with it. Anyway, I like you fine. If this turns into another fight I just want to be sure that you're on my side." He knew that he'd better change his tactics when he saw the quick gleam in the girl's brown eyes; it wouldn't do to let her get any wrong ideas. "I think we've got two things happening out here in the valley. Somebody's trying to run guns to the Indians and somebody else is making a try at getting some kind of plunder out of the Confederacy. Maybe the two attempts are mixed up with each other. Likely enough some of these wagon people are doing it. I'd just like to know who and what I'm up against."

"Sorry," she said, giving him that look again. "Ah ain't seen nothin' that'd help."

"Just keep watching. I'll talk to you later."

Partly to make it seem that he was moving away for some perfectly valid reason he took time to get cleaned up and shaved. After a week on the trail, the last two days without even time for a decent wash, he felt rather disreputable. It was only when he had a clean, smooth face once more that he wondered if shaving hadn't been a mistake. He didn't want Susie to think that he had done it on her account. There was no good in giving the girl ideas. Maybe she already had too many.

When he joined the group once more they seemed to have improved their dispositions a little, joking about his improved appearance. It didn't last long, however. All of them were too anxious about their predicament. They wanted to know what their somewhat unwilling leader was planning to do.

"Not too much we can do right now," he explained. "It seems like a safe bet that this gang ahead of us is the Maddigan outfit. We know that they want to get their hands on Mellew—for some reason or other. They know that we're here because Jed must have told them by this time. But they don't know much about us. Jed couldn't have told them how many were in the force that broke up the ambush. I think Maddigan will try to look us over first and then try to suck us into an ambush that he'll set up. He'll have it figured out that we don't know he's there and he'll think that the ambush plan is the safest way for him."

"What does that mean to us?" Jakes asked.

"It keeps them thinking for a while. We've got to stick around for at least another day or two while Susie's wound begins to heal. Maybe we can use the time to confuse them some more. They won't know why we're waiting but they'll hope that we'll walk into their trap. So they won't be in any big hurry to make a move." He didn't add that he was banking on his belief that Maddigan wanted to arrange a meeting with Garnsey and would have to make his moves with that in mind. He wasn't too sure what it might mean and anyway he preferred to keep that idea to himself for a while.

"So we delay," Jakes persisted. "What does it get us? Things won't get any better."

"There's always a chance. Somebody else might start moving along this trail. Maybe we can arrange a truce and see what they want."

"Meanin' you'll turn me over to 'em?" Mellew growled. "What if it ain't me they want?"

"Who else would it be?" Garnsey inquired sarcastically.

"You, damn you! I think you made a deal to have Maddigan run them stolen muskets to the Indians. Maybe he wants to get paid."

"That's ridiculous!"

"The hell it is. You're the man who done a hell of a lot o' talkin' about stirrin' up the redskins against the Union. Maybe if it was your wagon what got searched there might be somethin' to give us a hint."

Garnsey started to sputter but Hale cut him off. "I think that's a fair idea. We searched Mellew's outfit. I think we'd better make a complete job of it."

"You're insolent, Captain Hale!" the little man shouted. "I won't have it! My wagon contains nothing but the merest trinkets needed to establish good relations with the Indians."

"Then there's no reason why we shouldn't have

a look. Mr. Shattuck, do you have any objections to a search of your wagon?"

The tall man shook his head and Hale turned toward Old Ben. "Sergeant Tolliver, take the Garnsey wagon. I'll have a look at Shattuck's."

Susie caught his eye as he went across to the big vehicle. "Gettin' real brash, ain't yo'?" she inquired with a sly grin. "Shavin' off them ugly ole whiskers kinda brung out the vinegar."

"Just doing my job," he retorted, not meeting her eyes.

"Want to search this bunk fust?" she inquired. "Ah ain't nevah been searched by a purty Ranger."

"Stop talking like a slut!" Shattuck howled at her. "Damned if'n I know what I'm ever gonna do with you!"

Hale saw that her smile had faded into a quick frown of rebellion so he said quietly, "Don't worry your uncle, Susie. He's got enough troubles on his mind." Then he climbed into the wagon and began to rummage around through the various boxes and bales.

It didn't take long for him to decide that Mr. Golightly Shattuck had told only the truth about himself. His trade goods were just what both he and Susie had claimed them to be, the cheap odds and ends procurable behind the blockade. There were no hidden spaces, no boxes with false packing.

He went out again, aware that a tense silence

had fallen on the group near the Garnsey wagon. Tolliver was sitting on the wagon seat with an open box beside him and a gun in his hand.

"What did you find?" Hale asked as he strode across.

"Ca'tridges, Cap'n. Twelve boxes half full of 'em."

Jakes broke out with an expression of surprise but then rasped a question at Ben. "Why didn't you say so at first instead of sitting there with your gun out and a fool look on your face?"

Tolliver stared back without expression. "Sounds like ye ain't too happy, Mister. Could it be ye had a hand in this business?"

"Hold it, both of you!" Hale ordered. "Let me have a look at what's in there. After that I'm going to want some answers. I'll get them if I have to beat them out of somebody! Keep your gun ready, Ben."

Chapter 9

Hale climbed past Tolliver into the ambulance, seeing that Ben had pulled apart what appeared to be the bedding Jakes and Garnsey had used. Apparently blankets had been spread on top of a flat layer of boxes which neatly filled up the wagon's floor space. One box had been removed from the layer but none of the others had been opened.

"Did you look into any of the other boxes?" Hale asked over his shoulder.

"Nope. One box was enough to tell me I oughta let ye handle the rest of it. There's a hatchet here on the seat if'n ye want to look at any more."

Hale reached for the hatchet and went to work, opening four boxes to find that all of them had been packed in the same manner. On top was a layer of trade goods such as calico, cheap hatchets or knives, but underneath would be a quantity of paper cartridges. Probably three quarters of the total bulk was made up of cartridges, always separated from the other goods by a layer of canvas that served as a false top for the deadly loads.

Hale put several of the cartridges into a pocket and then crawled back to join Tolliver. He took his place on the seat of the wagon and stared at the waiting men in front of him. "Things begin to add up more and more," he said slowly. "A man named Maddigan steals guns from a warehouse. He brings them out here, swinging up into the Nations to keep clear of any pursuit by the law—and maybe to pick up a few extra outlaws to help him. Now he's up the river—and we know what he's waiting for. Ammunition for the guns. Like Ryan, he'd be willing to kill a lot of people to get that ammunition."

He pulled out a few of the cartridges and held them up for the others to see. "Buck and ball cartridges. Just the thing for raw recruits or Indians who can't shoot straight. What about it, Garnsey? Was the deal that you'd turn the cartridges over to Maddigan or that he'd deliver the guns to you? Or maybe is this the spot where he gets paid for helping you handle the whole deal?"

"I don't know anything about it!" the little man screamed. "I didn't know there was anything like that in my wagon. I think you just put them in there to make me look bad."

"Sure," Hale said with heavy irony. "I smuggled a few thousand of them into the wagon just now while everybody was looking. Come off it, Seymour! Your crazy scheme to stir up Indians hasn't been any secret. What's the deal with Maddigan? What is he waiting for up the river?"

"I tell you I don't know! I didn't put those

cartridges into the wagon. I didn't know they were in there. Somebody must have tampered with the load before I started west." The pompous surliness was no longer in the little man's tones. Now he was simply scared.

"How about it, Jakes?" Hale asked. "What do you know about it? Did you join up with him before or after the wagon had its load?"

"After. I took his word for it that the boxes under our bedrolls and baggage were simple trade goods. It didn't occur to me to pry any of them open and take a look."

"Let's get this straight. Garnsey, do you claim that you don't own these cartridges and that you don't know who does?"

"I certainly do!"

"Jakes! You make the same claim?"

"Sure. Only in my case it's the truth."

"He's a liar!" Garnsey yelled. "He planted them there!"

"Hold it! Both of you deny ownership. Is that right?"

Both men shouted affirmatives. Hale grinned thinly. "That's just what I wanted to hear, gents. Nobody owns the things. As a law officer I'm declaring 'em to be dangerous property of outlaw ownership. Best thing to do is to get rid of them where they won't cause any trouble. Start handing out the boxes, Sergeant Tolliver!"

There was a flat silence and then Mellew

laughed loudly. "Damned if he ain't pulled one over on somebody! Me, I'm glad I ain't mixed up in it."

"You are," Hale told him, taking the box Tolliver had first brought out and removing the trade goods from it. "You just got yourself appointed an honorary Texas Ranger. The appointment lasts long enough for you to lend a hand with these boxes. Grab this first one and head for the river. When you get to the edge of the mud flat start throwin' cartridges a fistful at a time. I want 'em spread all up and down the channel—under water."

Mellew seemed delighted to do the work. Jakes also decided to get into it, for what reason Hale could not be certain. Within a few minutes the Garnsey wagon contained only personal gear and a scattering of trade items. The boxes were still on the ground and the thousands of musket cartridges were on the bottom of the Red River. Two loads of them had been saved because it seemed that they would fit both Mellew's musket and Susie's carbine. With a probable fight coming up it didn't seem like a bad idea to have extra ammunition on hand.

Jakes sidled up to Hale when the job was done. "Captain, you don't think I had any hand in bringing those cartridges out here, do you?"

"Not interested," Hale told him curtly. "It's not important for me to figure out who the liars are. We're all in the same mess together."

"But I . . ."

"Forget it! I don't expect to trust anybody. Talk won't mean a thing unless we get out of this trap we're in."

He motioned to Tolliver and the pair of them went across to get their horses. Hale didn't say a word to anyone. He was thinking that the phrase he had used to Jakes was gloomily significant. They were in a trap. At a time when he ought to be doing something about intercepting that musket shipment he was tied down with a lot of people who probably weren't worth defending. He had to stick with them and find out just what kind of trouble actually threatened. Meanwhile he could do nothing about the stolen muskets except hope that Maddigan wouldn't move them until he had done whatever it was he proposed to do about these wagons on the riverbank.

When they were on the ridge, out of earshot of the others, Hale asked, "What did you think of those cartridges, Ben? Ever see any just like them?"

"Sure. They was the reg'lar buck-and-ball."

"Not quite. Three buckshot and a musket ball with each load of powder, all right, but not quite the kind of job I've been seeing."

"Kinda sloppy-made, mebbe."

"That and the caliber. I never happened on too much buck-and-ball stuff for the smaller caliber muskets like Harpers Ferry and Springfield.

Mostly they issued the things to green troops when they handed out the big bore muskets of older models. Men who didn't get much musket drill could still do a lot of damage when they pulled the trigger on that kind of a load."

"So ye figger a bunch o' Injuns what ain't no great shucks with a white man's gun could use the same kind o' things?"

"Seems reasonable. If somebody stole muskets for use in a proposed Indian uprising they would have to take the kind of guns available. I know that there must have been a lot of Springfields of one kind or another—and quite a few Enfields—tied up here just like those ambulances were blocked. So the stolen muskets would have been either fifty-seven or fifty-eight caliber arms. But there hadn't been much buck-and-ball used in that caliber in this part of the country since early in the war. I think somebody went to a lot of trouble to make up a lot of buck-and-ball cartridges to fit the stolen muskets. They wanted to make sure that the Indian renegades would do plenty of damage."

"It's crazy as hell!" Tolliver growled. "One way or another it's Texas that gits hell. Even if'n the redskins don't turn them guns on our folks we'll git the blame from the Yanks. And they're kinda in a spot to turn us inside out if' n they feel like doin' it."

"So we've got two chances. Either we get around Maddigan's gang and find the guns or we take a chance that he's going to come at us in a try at getting cartridges for the muskets."

"If'n that's what it is he wants."

"What difference does it make? Maybe Maddigan is trying to squeeze in a bit of gold hijacking with his gunrunning. Maybe he wants cartridges. Maybe Garnsey owes him money. It all works out the same way. He's out to get this wagon outfit. And that's what I've got to gamble on—that the guns won't be moved until he takes his whack at us."

"What was ye plannin' to do about that dam' Garnsey? He's the polecat what oughta be skinned alive!"

"You believe him? Or Jakes? Or Mellew?"

"I ain't sure I believe any of 'em."

"Same with me. I think they're all lying at some spot or other. The point is that we might need all of them. I don't know who to trust but I've got to figure that they'll all be useful simply because they don't dare try anything very crooked right now. Getting out of this mess will be a funny kind of a proposition, a lot of people who don't trust each other all having to help each other for selfish reasons. It could get interesting."

"Sure—and it could git damned nasty. When there's gold in the tale—no matter if'n it's real or not—men git mighty ornery."

"Funny thing," Hale told him. "I'm depending on that."

They were easing down from the ridge-end by that time, riding casually out into the open stretch that separated the two lots of hill country. If Maddigan proposed to scout the oncoming wagons he would have to send men out into this open patch. Meanwhile Hale wanted to let him know that the wagon party was still on hand. That had to be part of the strategy.

"How come ye're dependin' on orneriness?" Tolliver asked after spending a few minutes considering the younger man's remark.

Hale stared. Then he recalled his own statement. "I'm depending on Maddigan being greedy," he explained. "He's got that gunrunning game in front of him. Maybe he could make a good thing of it by double-crossing Garnsey and selling the guns to guerillas or outlaws. Maybe he'll try it anyhow. But meanwhile he's got other things that he wants. Maybe money, maybe ammunition. Maybe it's gold—or all three. I think that gold greed will keep him from making any move with the guns until he can have a try at stealing Mellew's loot."

"But Mellew ain't got it!"

"No matter. Maddigan thinks he has. Thousands of men have committed thousands of crimes for gold that didn't exist. You know that. When a man gets gold-crazy he does some pretty stupid things. That's what I'm hoping will happen here."

"Looks like ye're figgerin' right on one part of

it," Tolliver told him. "I'm guessin' that Maddigan and his gang is right where they was yestidday. Leastways they got a sentry out on that fust hill ahead of us. I jest seen him move."

"Good. Now we'll be reported. Let's ride on down into the bottom land and take a look at the trail the wagons will have to use."

"How come? What's the p'int in showin' ourselves?"

"I want things to look casual. Maddigan has to feel that the wagons stopped only because something in the fight yesterday caused delay. I want him to think that they'll move upstream almost any minute. If he thinks we're going to make the move maybe he won't make it."

"What's the idee o' delay? What's it goin' to git us?"

"Who knows? We can wait better than he can— because we know why we're waiting and he'll get itchy. Maybe we could prod him into a fool move. Now keep your eyes on the high country as we aim toward the river. I want to know what their sentry is doing. I'll look for sign of their having scouted down the river during the night."

It required only a few minutes to make a looping sweep of the flat country, remaining within sight but out of gunshot of the outlaw sentry. In that time they learned that no one had been along the river during the night. There was some show of movement in the timber up-river and Tolliver declared that one man was holding a sentry post on the north end of the next ridge while another man moved upstream as though going back to report.

"I don't git it," Old Ben complained. "How come they didn't have a scout out durin' the night?"

"One reason—I hope. They've decided to believe Jed. They know we're here and they want to make us come to them. If they're planning any kind of ambush they wouldn't spoil it by showing us tracks that would make us suspicious. So they didn't send out any scouts who'd make those tracks."

Old Ben grinned. "Soundin' like yerself more'n more all the time, Cap'n. What happens when they find out we ain't walkin' into their trap?"

"I don't know. But we'll keep them off-balance as long as we can. We're tied up with the wounded girl so we might as well use the time to worry them a little."

Tolliver grinned. "I kinda like the sound of it. I kin jest imagine that damned Maddigan. He wants to git his money outa the gun deal and he wants to git his paws on the gold he figgers Mellew's haulin'. He can't scarcely wait to make a grab but he figgers the safe game is to wait and toll us into a trap. It'll be a hell of a chore fer him to play the waitin' game his good sense tells him to play when his greediness is proddin' him to start makin' moves."

"Exactly the point of waiting," Hale nodded. "We'll try to out-guess his moods. Wait as long as we can. When he starts to move we'll try to move also, making it look as though we still didn't know he was around. Maybe we can fake him back into his ambush again. I don't know how long we can keep it up but it seems like the only move. Sooner or later he'll get careless or something else will happen. We've got to hope that any change will be some kind of improvement for us."

"Like somebody comin' along the river?"

"Maybe. The peace party could have wound up their business by this time and be headed for home. Or a supply train might show up. One was planned, I think, although it's not likely to be along so soon. I think that our best bet is that the Yanks might push a small column into this part of the country. If the war's over now—as maybe it is—they could start troops right up the valley of the Red. Or they might come right down through the Nations from the Colorado-South Platte country. After the fighting they had up there last fall they might try to bust things up all through the Indian Nations."

Tolliver grimaced, his whiskers brushing his thin chest as he wagged his head. "It don't sound like no real good chance, Cap'n. Ye better hope that Susie gal kin git around to handlin' a gun. I'm thinkin' she'll be wuth any two of the others in a scrap."

"I'm not planning to use her."

"Ye won't have no choice, Cap'n. That gal's got a mind of her own. And don't fergit that she's got eyes. Ye're kinda purty without yer whiskers, ye know. I seen the way she was lookin' at ye."

"I'm not interested."

"Don't git stand-offish. She's yer best lot o' troops right now. There ain't no point in makin' her sore by givin' her the cold shoulder. Like the Good Book says, "Hell ain't got no fury like a woman's corns—or somethin' like that.""

Hale kept his face straight. "I'll try to remember your advice, Sergeant. Maybe we can get the lady sore and then aim her at the enemy."

"Don't git careless about it; the gal's got her eye on ye."

"Don't worry. I don't think it means a thing. It looks to me as though she's a girl who's been kept down a lot. Her uncle hates to admit that she's a woman now and she resents it. I think she tries to shock him once in a while because that's the only way she knows to show her rebellion. I happen to be handy for that purpose."

There was a surprise for them when they returned to camp. Hale said nothing about gold, guns, or cartridges. He simply outlined his plans for outwaiting Maddigan and found that his loudest supporter was Seymour Garnsey.

The little man announced pompously, "I'm for whatever Captain Hale wants. He's in charge here and it's up to him to figure out the proper strategy. Once we get out of this trouble it will be time enough to look into the charges that have been made."

Mellew jeered. "Kinda changin' yer tune, eh, Garnsey? More scared o' yer skin than yer reputation?"

Garnsey became more pompous than ever. "Sir, I am an accredited agent of the State of Texas. I have the documents to prove it—although no one seems interested in examining them. I also happen to know that Captain Hale is what he professes to be, a man with an outstanding war record who now is undertaking a most difficult assignment. I am depending on him to get at the truth of this dastardly plot against peace and against my own good name."

Hale asked quietly, "Are you claiming that you did not know about the cartridges being in your wagon?"

"Of course! Some scoundrel obviously removed some of my trade goods and substituted those bullets and powder. I was to be used as an unknowing tool for the villain behind this whole plot. Probably the gunrunners would be advised to murder me out here in the wilderness and thus get hold of the ammunition."

"Anything sounds possible after all that's been happening," Hale conceded. His private opinion was that Garnsey had found time to think up a pretty clever explanation. "Do you have any idea who it was who substituted cartridges for cotton?"

"Naturally. This man who calls himself Albert Jakes came to me as a stranger, asking for passage to the Washita. He had ample opportunity to make the switch."

"You're a liar!" Jakes shouted. "I never even looked into those boxes. You can't turn your own doings off onto me!"

"Forget it!" Hale snapped. "This is not a court. I don't care why a gang of outlaws was out to kill Chris Mellew. I don't care who loaded the cartridges. I don't even care very much who sent the guns or who stole them in the first place. Right now the only thing that counts is that we're faced with a gang of tough thugs who seem determined to wipe us out. Maybe they want one thing or maybe they want another. It's not important. We've got to stand together—and I expect to have my orders obeyed. Anybody who doesn't want to operate that way can hitch up and start moving. Take your own chances, if that's the way you want it. The rest of us might benefit."

Nobody made a move or said a word.

"Same routine as yesterday," he told them after a long pause. "We won't post any guard on the upstream side but somebody will be on the ridge opposite the wagons. Let them work down this way and take a look, if they want to. Just make sure that no attack gets started without our having

133

plenty of warning. Set the guard details, Jakes. Sergeant Tolliver and I need some sleep; we'll be doing most of the night job again."

"How long does this last?" Jakes asked.

"Maybe another day, depending on what the enemy does. Like I told you, I'm trying to out-guess their timing, hoping for some kind of a break in our favor. If nothing happens that will improve our position we might get some advantage out of having them a bit confused. It's a long shot, but we don't seem to have anything else."

He watched them set about their various chores, Garnsey climbing the ridge to take on the first bit of sentry duty while Jakes began to take the stock to the river for watering. Betsy made a show of sitting on the seat of the Mellew wagon with some mending in her lap. Mellew turned to some deft repair work on a piece of harness and Hale remembered that the man had been a sail-maker and ship's carpenter before becoming the Penelope's mate. Shattuck worked at collecting driftwood from the river's edge for the cooking fires. All of them were trying hard to seem casual about it but the tension was there. He realized that this waiting game might possibly backfire. These people might crack under the strain before Maddigan would.

When he awoke, only partly refreshed in the blistering heat that had settled on the valley, he knew that matters were getting worse. They had begun to wrangle among themselves over petty affairs and Garnsey seemed to be the principal object of ill-feeling. Hale didn't interfere. He could take a certain amount of grim pleasure out of hearing the little man getting blamed for everything from Confederate defeat to the flies which had begun to infest the camp.

He took a quick look at preparations for the night and then went over to where Betsy was talking with Susie. "How's the patient?" he asked.

"Not patient at all—if you can stand a bad joke," the blonde woman told him. "She wants to get up."

"Too soon. I'm hoping she'll be able to stand some travel tomorrow. Tonight she'd better get ready for it."

"Ah'm ready raht now," Susie declared. "This ole wound ain't nothin'."

"It's bad enough so that you could have a lot of trouble if you didn't take care of it."

"But Ah'm doin' fine. It don't hurt much."

"That's not the point. One bad move could open it up and then we'd be right back where we started. I want you ready to move when the time comes."

"Ah'll take it real easy, Cap'n," she promised. "Ah jest don't like gittin' babied all the damn time. Yo're wuss than Uncle Golly."

"For your own good. Keep that in mind. Anyway, tonight I'm depending on you to be guard officer. If your nurse says it's all right we might even let you get up and do the job on your own. That much moving around might not do any damage."

She closed her eyes, the smile on her lips again making him think of a brash young urchin who had been caught with his hand in the jam pot. "Ah'll git all rested up fer it," she promised.

Chapter 10

In spite of the wrangling there was no confusion about the real duties of the camp. Somebody had set up the rotation of sentries and Hale did not ask questions. They had arranged it so that he and Tolliver had the shift just at dusk but did not go on duty again until just before dawn. That was the way he wanted it.

There was no sign of movement up-river when darkness arrived and he went back to camp, Jakes taking his place on the hill. He found Susie in a blanket by the dying fire so he went across to ask, "Who set up the sentry duty?"

"Me. Who else. Did yo' say Ah was the officeh?"

"I just thought I'd ask. Good job. You're sure you'll be all right here?"

"Ah'm fit an' able."

"Keep it that way. Remember what I asked you to do about keeping your eyes open? Spot anything out of the way?"

"Nothin' Ah could put a fingah on. That Garnsey-Jakes combination has been doin' one hell of a lot o' jawin'."

"Natural enough," he told her with a thin smile. "I'll turn in now. Call me if there's even a hint of trouble."

"How 'bout if'n Ah git lonesome? Mebbe Ah oughta call yo' fer that?"

"Not unless you want Uncle Golly mad at both of us. Now behave yourself!"

The night passed quickly for him, a second good sleep helping to take most of the accumulated weariness out of his bones. When Susie roused him at the appointed hour for the dawn shift he felt a little better about the whole deal.

"All quiet," she reported. "Coffee on."

He stared at her in the darkness that was relieved only by the feeble glow of the fire. "You're not trying to do too much, are you?"

"Stop frettin' about me." For some reason she had dropped her air of deliberate impudence and seemed simply annoyed that he should concern himself. "Ah ain't wantin' all that sympathy jest because yo' figger it was part yore fault that Ah got hurt."

He wondered who had been talking to her during the night but he didn't think it would be smart to ask questions. Better to keep her thinking the way she was doing now. It would be easier all around.

He relieved Mellew on the ridge, learning that there had been no sounds of hostile movement during the night. The stocky man had turned sullen again, sleepiness adding to whatever else he had on his mind. Hale didn't waste time with him. "Get back to camp and catch yourself a few winks," he advised. "Forget that you're the one the gang seems to want; we're all in this together right now."

When he was alone he wondered about his own remark. Was it actually Mellew that Maddigan wanted? The stocky man had certainly been the target of the first attack but with Maddigan there were complications. Ryan could have assumed wrongly that Maddigan was trying to catch Mellew.

A few minutes later he heard movement below him and knew that Tolliver was coming out from camp, following the river bank. That part had been planned last evening. At dawn they would move out together, ready to spot any dawn attack that might be forming. Stirring up the enemy at a distance from the camp would give the wagoners a better chance to get ready.

He remained quiet until a changing in the tenor of the sounds around him warned that dawn was not far away. Insect noises began to give way to the first sleepy chirps of awakening birds and then the gray began to show on his left. As the stars faded out the birds became louder but no other sounds came to his straining ears.

Shadows gradually turned into bushes or clumps of distant trees. He could see the glint that was daylight reflecting on a bend of the Red. Then he saw something moving near the line of cotton-woods and knew that Old Ben was making his move.

He took a few cautious steps and halted again to listen and stare. Nothing was amiss. He moved forward once more, picking his cover with due care. It seemed pretty certain that Maddigan was not going to make any attack this morning but there was no point in getting careless. In this game a man couldn't afford to make even one mistake.

It took a good twenty minutes for him to reach the area where the ridge dropped away to flat prairie. The light was almost full by that time, the sun still below the horizon but likely to pop into view at almost any moment. Tolliver was angling in toward him now, showing that he had spotted his fellow scout. Ahead there was nothing but silent bottomland.

He was about to call out when he saw Ben go down on all fours to scan something along the line of cottonwoods. Hale promptly took over the lookout duty, holding his own position in readiness to cover Ben in case of surprise attack from the river.

Tolliver took only a moment and then started directly toward Hale. "They've started gittin' curious," the old man reported. "Looks like somebody rode down this fur some time durin' the night."

"He couldn't see much from here."

"This was where he left his hoss. I found boot marks fer another two hunnert yards or more. I reckon he seen what he wanted to see."

140

"One man only?"

"Yep."

"So they've made a move. Good."

"What's good about it?"

"I'm thinking about those guns. If Maddigan should decide that we're not worth bothering about he might get those wagons to some place where we couldn't find them. While he's here the guns won't move far."

"We can't figger him to stay patient much longer. If'n we don't make some kind of a move today he'll take the bit into his teeth."

"Let's head back to camp. I've got an idea. No use having to talk it through twice. You can hear it along with the others."

"Ye figger it's safe to go back and not leave nobody on watch?"

"I think so. They won't risk a daylight attack. Every move they've made—or haven't made— hints that they don't want to take risks. I think they'll keep operating that way, hoping to catch us foul."

They found a decent breakfast waiting for them this time. Shattuck had provided jam and some canned peaches. Betsy was doing better with her coffee and bacon. Hale explained his plan while he ate.

"They've begun to get restless. I think they'll try to hit us after dark if we stay where we are. And we're not in a good defensive position. There's too much cover on the ridge that they could use. I'd rather be out in the open."

"What if they hit us while we're moving?" Jakes asked. "We'll be in no position to fight because we'll have wagons and stock to handle."

"It's a risk—but I don't think it's a big one. Somehow I keep getting the feeling that Maddigan wants a lot in his favor before he starts anything. He went upstream quite a distance to set his ambush, letting Ryan get the jump on him. Now he's waited for another two days since Jed caught up with him. I think he'll keep trying to suck us into an ambush if he thinks there's a half decent chance of it working out that way."

"But it looks like you're taking us right into trouble," Mellew complained.

"That's what I'm hoping Maddigan will think. I think we should move out of here about noon. By that time the outlaws ought to be fixing up plans for a night attack. When they see us they'll go back to the ambush scheme—I hope. For what it may be worth we'll have them changing their minds a lot and it may make them open to a mistake or two. One way or another, we'll be in a better position to fight if we make a move up to that open stretch."

"Ye think it'll fool em?" Shattuck asked worriedly.

"We'll sure give it a try. I want our move to look like the start of a delayed day's march. Sergeant

Tolliver and I will ride out ahead just as though we were scouting for the party. I'll mark the spot in the open area where the wagons are to halt, but when you reach it you're to put on a show of having a breakdown of some kind. I'll leave that part up to you. Just make it look good. We want them to think that the halt will be only a short one."

"I get it," Jakes said in a more cheerful tone. "Let 'em think the ambush plan might still work. Don't let 'em guess that we know they're there."

They went over details until all of them knew what was expected. Then Hale went back up the river a short distance. The idea was to keep any of the outlaws from moving out into the open. Everything depended on the gang believing that their presence on the Red was undetected so he wanted to keep them hiding.

Tolliver relieved him after a short time and then Mellew took a turn. None of them rode far out into the flat country but simply let themselves be seen by outlaw sentries. At noon Hale gave the order to move and the three wagons began what appeared to be a routine march. Shattuck took the lead with a protesting Susie back in her bunk. Betsy had reported that the wound was doing quite well but that it still might reopen quite easily. It would be dangerous enough simply to ride and the best bet was to keep the girl flat as long as possible.

Hale saw them well started and left to ride ahead

with Tolliver, Mellew having been relieved from his patrol duty so that he could handle his wagon. Nobody offered any objection to any of his orders now. They were all tense enough but they were not wrangling.

Tolliver seemed to be particularly gleeful over the proposed strategy. "Seems like we oughta have 'em guessin' like mad," he told Hale when the two of them were well out ahead of the wagons. "Is this here the kind o' tricks ye worked on the Yankees?"

"You don't know much about my army experience, do you? I didn't have any chance to try much of anything in the strategy line."

"Right in the beginnin' ye was in plenty o' fightin', wasn't ye? They made ye a Cap'n, I know."

"Staff Officer. Errand boy. When they sent Ben McCulloch up to be second in command to General Sterling Price I went along as his aide. The rest of the Ranger Battalion didn't go and that was the last time I saw any of them. After the battle of Wilson's Creek I kept shuffling around from one army to another, always a sort of errand boy for somebody. No strategy for me."

"Too damned bad. This deal makes it look like ye'd ha' been mighty good at it."

"Wait and see. Maybe we don't fool them. Maybe fooling them won't help. Right now I don't see any way to cash in an advantage even if we get one. The whole mess keeps getting more tangled all the time. All we need is for some of those Indians up on the Washita to break loose and start back in this direction for some of their old-fashioned raids!"

Tolliver grinned. "It's gittin' ye down, Cap'n. Buck up!"

Hale nodded, smiling a little at his own show of pessimism. By that time the wagons were coming into view behind them as a bend of the river brought them out from behind the concealing ridge. Suddenly Ben exclaimed happily, "We stirred 'em up! That sentry on the hill d'rectly ahead of us jest lit a shuck outa there. Hustlin' off to report the wagons, I reckon."

"Good. Exactly what we want. Did you see more than one man?"

"Nope."

"Keep riding. We've got to act as though somebody else was still watching. There will be even if there isn't right now."

"Ye don't wanta stir 'em into takin' a shot at us, Cap'n."

"They won't. They don't think we know about them and they ought to be getting a bit excited now that they think we're moving into their ambush. Slow down a bit; we don't want to be too far ahead when the wagons reach the spot I marked."

Tolliver cackled happily. "This here's kinda fun,

Cap'n. I wish I could be close enough to see them polecats fixin' up their ambush. They'll be blottin' sign in a hell of a hurry. They won't know what the hell to think when the wagons pull up."

"I just hope you're right. If Maddigan will manage to lose his head and do something foolish we may gain a bit."

He was thinking about it as they rode on toward the next bit of high ground. It was fine to talk about taking advantage of the trick they were playing on the enemy, but the stark fact was that the odds were still bad. The wagon party was out-numbered, outgunned, and probably incompetent for any real fight. There was even a chance that some member of the company might prove traitorous at a critical moment. Both Mellew and Garnsey had been suspiciously cooperative during the past few hours.

"Looks like it might be fixin' to weather up a mite," Old Ben observed. "There's a bit of dark showin' over there in the nor'west. We might git some of it."

"Bad," Hale muttered. "If they jump us under cover of a storm we'd lose the advantage we gain by moving into the open."

Tolliver grunted assent and they moved on up-river toward the hills. Now they were risking double danger. There might be snipers on the ridge or among the willows by the river. Possibly the outlaws might decide to give up their ambush in favor of killing two of the wagon party in a hurry.

Hale cut it pretty fine, calling a halt only when they were almost within musket shot of the first good cover. He pulled up, looking back as though concerned about the wagons. The timing was good. The little train had halted and men were moving about on foot. The men were playing their part well so far. An observer would certainly have thought that there was some kind of wheel trouble on the big wagon.

"Time to go," Hale told Ben quietly. "You cut back at a run while I hold on here for a minute or two. I'll keep an eye open to see whether your move stirs up any action."

Old Ben started to protest but Hale waved him around. The little man obeyed and Hale scanned the willows on the ridge. Nothing moved. Apparently the lookout had been alone before he left his post to ride back and report the wagon movement.

Hale remained motionless until he caught a flicker of movement farther upstream. Somebody was coming down to take a look. He turned his horse slowly, waiting to give the enemy plenty of time to spot him. Then he rode back a few yards and halted once more. He wanted to make it appear that he was undecided about going back to the wagons.

After a few minutes of careful maneuvering he

put his mount to an easy trot and headed for the wagons. An idea had come to him and he kept the pace easy so as to have time for some thinking. Maybe there was a better chance for the party than by sticking to this cat-and-mouse game.

The wagoners were waiting at the Shattuck wagon when he rode up. Mellew even went through some exaggerated motions as though reporting a breakdown. It was Garnsey who fired a real question.

"Do we go into defense position now or shall we go on with this playacting?"

"Keep right on with the show. You're doing fine. Leave the wagons just as they are. We want them to think that we might move again at any moment."

"What's the good of it?" Mellew demanded. "If we're going to fight we might as well get ready."

Hale slid from the saddle before making any reply. "I think maybe we've got a chance to keep out of a fight. See that black streak in the west. If it's the kind of storm I think it is it'll likely come this way. Most such storms do—and we've had just the kind of weather to bring one."

"What's that got to do with it?" Mellew was showing the old belligerence again. "All the more reason to get ready for double trouble."

"Keep quiet a minute and you'll see what I'm driving at. Right now I think we've got the enemy guessing. They expect us to move on into their trap as soon as we get a repair job done. If we start making camp they'll know different. They might change their plans and move in on us. If they keep on expecting us to move they'll sit tight. At least that's what I'm hoping."

"We can't keep 'em fooled forever," Jakes put in.

"Let me finish. You're forgetting about this storm."

"No I'm not! I'm thinking that a storm would give them just the chance they need to close in on us."

Hale stared him down. "Have you spent any amount of time in this country, Mr. Jakes?"

"No."

"Then let me tell you something about it. Storms out this way get mighty ornery. One minute the Red's a lot of mud flats and then it's suddenly bank full. A real old gully-washer west of here can start a flash flood when there's no rain along this stretch of river. I've got a hunch that somebody upstream is getting a lot of rain right now—and I'm hoping that it's not too close."

Puzzled glances told him that the point still wasn't clear to them. "It's a long chance and we'll need some luck for the time to work out the way we want it but it's a better gamble than anything else that's open to us. Suppose the rain hits here? Maybe by late afternoon or tonight. The river will rise in a hurry. It could start rising without rain if there's enough of a storm to the west of us. What

I'm hoping is that we can duck back to the ford under cover of darkness or storm and get across to the north side without having Maddigan know what we're doing. It'll be rough but we might get away with it. If we're real lucky they won't know we've moved until the river gets too high for them to follow us. Now do you see why I want them to think that we'll be moving on upstream any minute now?"

"Sounds good," Jakes nodded. "Sorry I sounded critical. Just call the shots and we'll try to handle the deal."

Chapter 11

Hale issued his orders crisply while his hearers were in a mood to accept them. At all times a couple of men would be moving around at the Shattuck wagon, continuing with a show of repairing a broken wheel. Those not busy with that duty would take care of the other preparations for a quick move. At all times a rider would be moving around in the flat area ahead. That would keep the outlaws at a distance and under cover, letting them see only what the wagoners wanted them to see.

"Get everything fastened down in your wagons," he warned them. "Lash everything down. We may have to cross the river after the rise has started and we'll likely get pushed around plenty. Take all precautions."

"Storm's gittin' closer," Old Ben observed. "Supposin' it hits us before we're ready?"

"Stop fussin'!" Susie's voice broke in from her place in the big wagon. "Can't yo' see the Cap'n's doin' enough worryin' fer all of us?"

There was a quick laugh from the group. It was a nervous sort of laugh but Hale liked the sound. They appreciated the humor because they were accepting the truth behind it. Somehow this seemed to be an entirely different lot of people than the lot who had fretted and wrangled at the other camp. Down there he had been trying to do something for an odd collection of rogues, sharpers, and malcontents. Now things had changed. Individuals had ceased to exist. Now there was a little group of people with a common cause and a common leader. They were depending on that leader to get them out of trouble.

"Keep in mind what we're trying to do," he warned them finally. "We keep the outlaws from getting a close look. That's the patrol's duty. Keep them thinking that we're going to move into their trap. When it begins to get dark, Sergeant Tolliver will take the patrol duty while we hustle the wagons back to the ford and get them across the river. The move will have to be timed just right—if the weather lets us have our way. If we start too soon, or give our intentions away too soon, they'll know what we're doing. Just play it cozy."

"Won't we be in danger when we get across to the Indian side?" Shattuck asked.

"No more than this side. For us the safe side is the one that the Maddigan gang is not on. Indians we can forget—I hope. For travel purposes it won't make much difference; we'd be crossing before long if we followed the proposed trail to the Washita. For my purpose it's the best side; that's the side where those ammunition and gun wagons are hidden. I hope."

"I got a idee," Old Ben told him. "When ye

move the wagons back why not leave a couple o' fires burnin'? Make the varmints think we're still settin' here."

"Smart idea," Jakes approved. "You're a genius, Sergeant."

"Jest got a good memory," Tolliver grinned. "That's the trick Gen'ral Washin'ton used on the British at Valley Forge or some place like that."

Hale laughed. "Don't tell me Benjamin Franklin told you about that!"

It was evident that the others didn't understand the humor but there was no time to explain. Susie's voice broke in again. "It was Princeton," she announced. "An' ah got another idea to go with it. If them bandits kin see fiahs they could likewise see that theah ain't no wagons near the fiahs. Let's put up somethin' that'd look like wagons in the dahk."

"'Nother dam' genius," Tolliver cackled. "Mebbe canvas on poles could do the trick."

Mellew threw in a suggestion. "I got a good axe among my tools. Suppose I get up there on the ridge and cut poles? It's a good plan."

"I'll cut the poles," Hale told him. "I'll do it while I'm riding a scout circle around the wagons. Then they won't see anything we don't want them to see. Mellew, I've got another job for you. You're a sailor who knows how to build things. Can you rig up a sort of harness that will let us make a quick hitch to use extra horses? We may have to unhitch in a hurry and bring the spare horses back to use on other wagons."

"I can do it," the stocky man said quickly. "Another good stunt."

"So get at it. Long lead lines with a quick hitch. You'll know what to do."

That was the way it went through the hot afternoon. Wagons were checked carefully for the crossing. Poles were cut and canvas was taken from the boxes where once it had been used to hide the smuggled cartridges. The Garnsey wagon was almost empty now and Hale came up with another idea.

He went across to where Susie had spent the time grumbling about her own idle situation. She had slept most of the morning after her night's vigil and just before the first wagon move Betsy had tried to make her comfortable for the first bit of travel, getting her into a thin cotton dress that would avoid the use of a blanket. Now Hale had to ignore the way the dress outlined every fine curve of her body. "Rested up?" he asked briefly.

"Plenty. Ah could git up right now. Belle says the wound's doin' fine. Didn't hurt it a bit when Ah was up last night."

"Let's give it every chance. Another day should see the worst danger past. Meanwhile you've done your share so don't fret."

"What share? That stupid ole idea about canvas wasn't much."

"It could help. But I wasn't talking about that. You handled night duty and you helped to save the wagons in the first fight. Maybe you could do it again if we get into more trouble. I'm depending on you to be fit."

She was staring at him with an expression he could not completely interpret. There was perplexity in it but there was also satisfaction. Then she murmured, "Ah wish Uncle Golly'd think that way. He don't evah figgah that Ah'm . . ."

"He'll come along. Now let's get to what I wanted to tell you. Before we start back I want you to change wagons. We'll fix up a place for you in the Garnsey ambulance. There's plenty of room now that we've thrown out those damned cartridges."

"Why?"

"A couple of reasons. This wagon's clumsy and heavy. It could get into trouble if the crossing's bad. Lightening the load would help."

"So Ah'm jest extry weight, am Ah?"

"Don't get proddy. I said there were a couple of reasons. The big one is a matter of safety. This wagon could turn over mighty easy. I don't want you to get trapped in this oat bin if the wagon should go over. You'd drown, sure as hell."

"Thanks, Cap'n," she said softly. "Ah didn't figgah as how yo'd give a damn."

Hale fled. That tone had come back into her voice and he didn't want to encourage her.

Obviously she had been bullied by her worried uncle to the point where she was ready to snap at any show of appreciation or care. It was no time to let things get any more tangled than they were.

The intense heat became worse as the sun sank toward the top of the cloud bank and Tolliver began to make guesses as to when the weather change would strike them. They could almost see the clouds gathering force and the entire company bustled around in the stifling atmosphere, sweating out preparations for the move which might solve their problem.

There was some relief when the sun dropped behind the black clouds but then Hale gave the order to unhitch the waiting teams. With the afternoon almost gone and a storm racing toward them there was no point in continuing the first line of deception. Outlaw scouts would realize that the wagons would make no further progress today so it seemed wise to give the impression that the party was preparing to settle down for a bad night. It gave the drivers a chance to water the stock and still left the right impression on the watchers.

Meanwhile Hale was keeping a wary eye on the little channel which ran lazily between the mud flats. When the sun disappeared there was still no hint of rising water. For the first time he allowed himself to doubt his own plans. Maybe this storm wouldn't bring the rain he had hoped for. Maybe the Red would not rise at all.

Still he went on with preparations, getting everything set for a fast move. Crossing the river still seemed like good strategy regardless of whether rising water would block pursuit. The guns were on the other side and that was still the main objective.

Betsy had measured and cut the canvas that would go into two screens. Mellew was finishing the make-shift harnesses that would permit saddle horses to aid the wagons at the ford. Shattuck had started digging holes for the poles. Hale had gotten brief amusement out of that. Somehow there was a moral lesson involved, Hale thought quizzically, a stern old man taking orders from a woman like Betsy Appleby ought to mean something. She had told him where to dig and he was digging. Neither of them seemed to care that a hard storm would make the whole effort useless.

Hale made certain that the extra ammunition was divided between the Mellew and Shattuck wagons where there were weapons to fit it. When that was done he moved Susie over to the Garnsey ambulance, carrying her most of the way. Since she had been out of her bunk a couple of times during the afternoon—as well as during the previous night—he knew that she was not as helpless as she was pretending. He simply made her as comfortable as possible, ignoring the irate grumblings of Golightly Shattuck. The old man knew well enough that his niece was throwing herself at Hale and he didn't hesitate to condemn her for it.

Betsy was only a little more discreet. When Susie was in position to travel the blonde woman swung in beside Hale and murmured, "Seems like the pigeon is kinda taken with you, Captain. You might do worse."

"Shut up! I'm not interested."

"Like I said, you could do worse. She's rather cute—and with that figure of hers she'd be mighty attractive with a bit of grooming. I think I'll keep an eye on her. She might . . ."

"You let her alone! Maybe she's a damned fool about some things but don't make her worse!"

Betsy gave him a crooked smile and walked away to help with supper. "So you're not interested, eh?" she remarked over her shoulder.

"Hell!" Hale growled to himself. "I don't know whether I'm trying to save bodies or souls! I wish I'd gone right after those gun wagons in the first place. It would have been a lot simpler."

They ate their meal early, letting the distant watchers assume that they were simply trying to beat the storm but knowing that this might be the last chance at decent food for some time to come. All of them were silent now, watching the black sky and waiting for Hale to give the word. They were ready.

And the storm was really coming down on them. The first signs had been in the river channel. The current began to show traces of mud and then bits of grass and dead stick floated past. Before supper was over they could see whole tree branches with the green leaves still on them. Somewhere the wind was doing a lot of damage.

"Plenty of wind and not too far away," Hale commented. "And the current's beginning to pick up. I hope we can make our start before it gets too bad." An hour earlier he had been fearful that the storm would not materialize but now his fear was in the opposite direction. If it came too soon they would have to risk observation. With a good two hours of daylight left the timing was going to become critical.

Mellew had just gone out to relieve Tolliver on scout duty when the first giant raindrops began to pelt the camp. Ben was soaked to the skin when he came in for supper but he made no attempt to get at the slicker roll behind his saddle. "Ain't no use," he replied when Jakes asked him about it. "We're gonna git ourselves plenty wet and we're gonna stay that way fer a spell. Might as well git used to it."

He grimaced at Hale when the younger man stopped beside him. "Things is workin' out, Cap'n. The river's comin' up real fast now. Think we kin git across in time?"

"We'll have to," Hale replied grimly. "Maybe we won't be able to wait for night but we'll make the move even if we can't fool the gang. With any luck we could defend the ford and keep them on this side until the river stops them."

"Might be easier that way anyhow. It's gonna be a hell of a chore to find that sand bar in the dark."

"We'll find it. Jakes has already gone down the river to mark it while it's still above water. He'll be our guide."

"Damned if'n ye don't think of everything, Cap'n! Which ain't bad fer a man what didn't wanta think o' nothin' less'n a week ago."

Hale left him then, moving down to the edge of the river for another look. The current was violent already and the brown flood was beginning to wash out across the flats. What was more alarming was the amount of debris that was being swept along. Even a few small cottonwoods rolling along in the water attested to the violence of the distant storm. Things were getting worse by the minute. The storm was almost upon them.

Even as he turned back toward the wagons a blast of cold air brought a fresh downpour of rain. Darkness seemed to settle over the valley as though a blanket had been thrown across it. Hale made his decision at once. Visibility had become so bad that there was no need to wait for night. Even if the outlaw sentinels had not already ducked for cover they would not be able to see what the wagoners were doing. It was time to start. Maybe it was even past time.

He went back to the camp at a run, head down to

the storm. "Hitch 'em up!" he shouted. "Don't waste a second!"

Ben had swallowed the last of his coffee, sheltered by the big wagon. "I'm on my way," he yelled back. "I'll send Mellew in and foller when I figger ye're in the clear."

Suddenly the tense waiting was over and everyone was busy. Hale considered abandoning the screen project but decided to go ahead with it. In case the storm should blow over in a hurry it would be worth something to have the extra effort made. He saw that Betsy was bringing up Mellew's team so he took over the pole planting himself, carrying the pieces of canvas to a handy spot and weighting them down with rocks. Time was becoming mighty important.

Mellew galloped in just as he was getting the final pole into place but there was no need for more talk. Everybody knew what was expected and everybody was doing it.

Shattuck's wagon wheeled in a wide circle and disappeared into the pelting rain. Hale saw that the others were following so he kept right on with his chore. It was beginning to look like a foolish gesture now but they would need any help it might give them.

Suddenly he realized that he had a helper. Betsy Appleby staggered against him with her arms full of canvas. She was having a battle to hold the stuff but she didn't falter.

He reached out to take it, yelling above the howling gale, "Get back to your wagon. I'll do this."

"Let me help. It'll take both of us to hold it. I brought a hammer and I've got nails in my apron pocket." She was as thoroughly soaked as any of the others, her dress plastered against her body and her hair streaming in the wind. "I'll hold it while you drive nails. I'll hand them to you."

He didn't argue. She had organized the job and she was right about his need for assistance.

Hailstones began to sting their faces as they struggled to get the first nails into place but they hung on grimly, finally securing the first edge. Then the really hard part began. With both of them using every ounce of strength they could muster it was still almost impossible to keep the canvas from being torn from their grasps. Twice they lost it, nails tearing out so that they had to be replaced.

Somehow they finally managed to put one strip into place, both of them almost blinded by the stinging particles of ice. There was no certainty that the screen would stay up so Hale called it quits. "Let the other one go," he bellowed to the woman. "One will be enough—if it stays up. Let's get out of here before that sleet cuts us to ribbons."

Her only reply was to stagger across to where the second strip of canvas was threatening to break loose from the rocks that held it down. Bundling it in her arms she fell in beside him, trying to throw the makeshift tarp over both sets of shoulders. With it protecting their necks they could still feel the sting of the hailstones but now it wasn't quite so painful. If either of them thought about how chummy they must look with their arms around each other neither of them commented. Talking was getting to be difficult. They simply sloshed along through the mud in the direction the three wagons had gone.

Chapter 12

They had gone perhaps forty rods when a violent blast tore the canvas from them and sent it sailing into the murk. Neither made any move to chase it. Hale simply yelled in the woman's ear, "Keep your head down; the worst of it's behind us now."

Once more they helped each other along, dodging the whipping branches that lashed at them as the cottonwoods swayed to the fury of the gale. Bits of debris as well as hailstones pelted their backs. The mud made running a difficult business. In the darkness they almost broke through the line of cottonwoods and into the mud area but Hale got his bearings in time, mostly because he could hear the roar of the river above the shriek of the wind. Finally they almost ended the dash in disaster when they collided with the back of Garnsey's wagon where it had halted to await its turn at the crossing. Hale took most of the collision, grabbing Betsy to keep her from a full crash against the wagon.

"You all right now?" he shouted down at her when he was sure she hadn't been injured. "Hustle right on around and climb in with Mellew. I've got to get up there and give Jakes a hand."

He didn't wait for her reply but splashed on through the mud past the frightened horses that were at the tail of the Mellew wagon. He knew that Betsy had swung around the animals and was approaching the ambulance seat so he paid no further attention to her. Mellew yelled something out of the gloom but Hale couldn't make out the words and did not bother to ask for a repeat. The roar of the river was quite enough to warn him that there was no time for delay of any kind. The Red was running in full flood. Every minute could be critical.

He saw Jakes coming up out of the ford with two horses behind him. The lean man bawled a report out of the storm's fury. "I got your horse and another one. Used 'em both to get the big wagon across. Goin' to need 'em on Mellew's. It's getting mighty bad out there."

Hale climbed into his own saddle and shouted a reply. "Hook up your pony and the extra. Get going in a hurry. I'll be right behind you with the Garnsey wagon. We can't risk taking turns now."

"Is Tolliver with you?"

"Not yet. We can't wait for him; the river's rising by the minute."

"Gear's on your saddle," the lean man howled. "Works real good. I'm on my way."

He disappeared into the darkness while Hale examined the lead ropes by feel. Then he went back to put the line on Garnsey's ambulance. It would hold, he thought. Mellew's seamanship was coming in pretty handy.

There was time for him to have a fleeting thought that he was getting pretty good service out of a lot of people he did not trust, but then he was shouting his orders to the huddled form on the driver's seat. He could only hope that Garnsey would rise to the occasion as the others seemed to be doing.

The little man was to drive straight into the river, following the Mellew wagon while it was still visible. Jakes should know the crossing by this time. They would have to depend on him because everybody had to do a bit of blind following. The trick would be to keep Mellew in sight without getting the team tangled up with the extra horses at the rear of the Mellew ambulance. Any kind of mix-up in mid-stream would be fatal. Hale would try to stay above the last wagon, using his horse to hold the ambulance against the side pull of the flood. It wasn't going to be easy.

By the time the extra line was made fast Mellew was moving. Hale swung back into his saddle, yelling at Garnsey, "Start 'em moving. Don't stop for anything—and don't lose your head!"

They wheeled out across the submerged mud flat in good shape, the frantic horses giving Garnsey a bit of trouble as he tried to keep a pace that left him close behind Mellew. There was no way to distinguish between mud flat and channel now. Hale knew they were actually in the river only when he sensed that there was more water under the horse than in the air—which didn't seem quite possible. It was raining so hard that at times he wasn't even sure that he could see his bronc's ears.

He pulled ahead a little, trying to make sure that they were following Mellew properly. Garnsey was yelling shrill curses above the howl of wind and water and Hale knew that the wagon must be getting a heavy pounding from the current. All of the horses were having trouble keeping their feet. He tried to angle upstream a little more so as to provide a better anti-current drag on the ambulance but quickly realized that his horse was getting into deep water above the actual ford. When he eased off to the proper line the rope slackened alarmingly and he knew that he was giving Garnsey no help.

Before he could send his horse ahead into a more efficient effort the animal stumbled and almost went down. Hale had a moment's vision of both of them being swept down in the flood but then the horse recovered and the rope tightened again. The water was shoaling a little. They must be out of the channel and at the edge of the sandbar.

Then he felt the horse lurch again. This time it was a different sort of motion. The bronc had not stumbled but was being hauled backward by a heavy pull on the wagon rope. Somehow Garnsey had let himself get into the main channel and his wagon was sliding downstream.

There were agonizing moments that seemed like hours as the horse fought to keep his feet but then another rider swung in to get a hold on the straining rope and relieve some of the pressure. Hale could sense rather than see that it was Ben Tolliver. The little man had arrived just in time.

Between them they managed to halt the slippage but Hale knew that the wagon silhouette was now different. Tolliver yelled a shrill warning even as Hale tried to catch his breath.

"Rolled over! We ain't got no chance of gittin' it out now."

Hale was moving as the words reached high. "Hang on hard!" he shouted at Old Ben. "Keep both broncs pulling!" Then he was going down the rope hand over hand. It seemed like the only way to reach the ambulance without being swept past it. If the whole outfit went . . . he didn't take time to think about it.

Garnsey's grays were struggling frantically to get rid of the weight that was dragging them backward into the wild river and Hale had to risk a tangle with them as he went past. At the same moment he glimpsed another type of shadow in the gloom. Garnsey was getting out of the mess by scrambling over the backs of the horses. Either he was abandoning Susie or the girl was already gone, perhaps swept out of the ambulance by the flood at the moment of disaster.

Hale didn't stop. He got a grip on the wagon seat

and knew that the wagon had toppled to its right side. Only a little of the left front corner was out of water, the current boiling around the way white water surged around rocks in a rapid. He guessed that the right wheels had begun to slide into deeper water at the lower rim of the sandbar and that had caused the wagon to tip over with the flood pushing it. Now it was hung precariously at the edge of the sand. It didn't seem possible that the horses could hold it there much longer.

He practically swam around the projecting end of the wagon seat, yelling Susie's name as loudly as possible. When his voice sounded louder in his own ears he knew that he was inside the wagon. At that moment his groping fingers found something that seemed like flesh so he took a firm grip and began to back out. He guessed that he had caught hold of Susie's wrist but there was not time to make certain. He had to get out before the wagon could take them both down the river.

It was a matter of sheer strength to work out into the open against the lash of the current and almost as big a problem to inch his way up the rope with the girl in the curve of one arm. She had not shown any sign of life since he'd found her so he didn't know whether he was saving her or simply taking a dead body ashore. Nor did he think much about it. The big idea was to get clear of this tangle and find something solid underfoot.

He released his hold on the rope when he felt

mud under his feet. "Try to hold!" he bawled in the direction of Tolliver's shadow. "I'll be right back." Somehow the storm had lightened a little. He could see objects more clearly.

It took a few shaky minutes to get out of the last stretch of shallow water but then he was bending to the storm and climbing a slope where cotton-woods posed a new menace to the inert figure in his arms. Suddenly he got help. Two men—Mellew and Jakes, he thought—took the girl from him and yelled something that he couldn't quite make out.

"Take care of her," he yelled back, turning back toward the river.

He was too late. Tolliver came up the slope with a horse behind him. "Had to cut it loose," he shouted when Hale blocked his way. "The dam' thing was about to drag us all in."

There was nothing to be said. It had happened. Hale simply took the reins of his mount from Old Ben and led the way through a break in the timber. Moments later they pulled up in the partial shelter afforded by the Shattuck wagon. The gale seemed to have subsided just a little and when Jakes came across to them they were able to talk in something more like normal tones.

"We got the girl in there," Jakes reported, pointing to the big wagon. "Inside, not in the cubby-hole. She's alive. Musta hit her head on something when the wagon went over, I suppose."

"Still unconscious?"

"The last I knew she was. Belle Mellew's with her. Seemed like she ought to handle the job. The girl might as well have been naked with nothing but that wet rag on her."

"I know. Did Garnsey get ashore?"

"He's babbling around here somewhere." Jakes sounded pretty disgusted. "I think he went into a panic and clawed his way out. He claims he didn't leave the wagon until he thought Susie was dead and beyond help. I don't believe a damned word of it."

"No matter. How's her wound? Hauling her around the way we did wasn't the easiest kind of treatment for a fresh hurt."

"Belle says it's all right. What do we do now?"

"We start reaching for higher ground. This spot could be under water by daybreak."

"Where'd you find Tolliver?"

"I didn't. He found me—and just in time to keep the wagon from going down the river with Susie in it. He's uncommon lucky with his moves. Go with him and see if his luck holds out in finding an opening through the timber. We've got to get the wagons to higher ground."

"There's a hole, all right," Old Ben said. "I recall it from that day when we rode down through here after gittin' our look at the Maddigan camp." He seemed quite elated at the left-handed compliment Hale had given him.

Both men moved away on foot, leading their horses. Hale tied his mount to a wagon wheel and took a quick survey of the position the wagons now occupied. Shattuck's oxen were firmly wedged into a sort of pocket of forest. Evidently the gangling old man had kept his team moving as long as he could, going blind and simply trying to get distance between the outfit and the river. When they could move no farther he had stopped. Now there would have to be some careful backing done before the big wagon could be swung around to head for the opening that Hale half remembered.

Mellew's wagon was no problem. His mules simply rested, heads down against the slackening rain. Hale saw that they could be turned in either direction so he went back to the big wagon, calling an inquiry into its dark interior. "All right to start moving this outfit?"

Betsy's muffled voice replied, "Any time. I've got her wedged in a mite with rolled blankets. They're wet but they'll do the trick. Just get us out of this miserable country!"

"Five minutes," he called back. "Is Susie still unconscious?"

"She's coming around. Maybe a bit of bumping will stir her some."

He found Garnsey in the Mellew wagon but he didn't bother to comment on what had happened at the crossing. He simply outlined plans for the balance of the night. Mellew was to lead off with his wagon now. Blundering along in the darkness might well get them into some sort of trap where the flood waters could overtake them. Mellew's ambulance was less vulnerable to such a risk so it was good sense to let the light wagon go ahead. Then any disaster to the big outfit wouldn't block everybody. Better to save one vehicle than to take an unnecessary chance on losing both.

Jakes and Tolliver came back while he was talking. They had found the trail, such as it was. It wasn't really a trail but simply an opening in the timber that they hoped would be wide enough for wagons. It led to higher ground and that was what they wanted. Hale put them to the task of getting the Shattuck wagon turned around and put his own efforts into getting Mellew clear of the maneuver. Things worked out smoothly enough. Within a matter of minutes they were moving again, Tolliver leading the way into the gap while Hale and Jakes saw to it that the extra stock didn't cause trouble.

The gap proved to be wide enough. It was rough and the rain had turned the slope into a slippery slant of mud but somehow they managed to make the climb. After a half hour of sweaty groping Hale began to feel a little better. A flash flood certainly wouldn't come this high. It annoyed him that he hadn't paid more attention to the terrain on his previous ride into this part of the country but annoyance was pretty well submerged in a different feeling. The trick had worked. The wagon company was on the north shore of the Red with a violent flood between them and the Maddigan gang. There were still all kinds of troubles ahead but for the first time it was not a matter of real emergency.

For the next couple of hours there was no time for a feeling of either triumph or dread. It was all they could do to keep the wagons moving. Twice there were substantial delays when Shattuck's oxen could not make a climb that Mellew's mules had negotiated without trouble. Each time the lighter wagon was halted while extra animals were put to the job of hauling the big wagon over the hump. On another occasion neither team could make the grade they found ahead of them and the scouts had to work out a detour that would take them around the timber on more level ground. By that time they had reached what Hale believed to be the crest of the northside ridge. The rain was coming down heavily once more although the worst of the wind seemed to have passed. Being wet no longer made any difference; it was just something they had learned to endure without expecting any quick relief.

"Get down and lead your team," Hale told Mellew finally. "Try to stay on the top of the ridge and keep moving in this same general direction. The rest of us will stick with Shattuck. Don't worry about making any great distance;

just stay on high ground away from the worst of that mud."

He joined with the others in helping the Shattuck outfit along, realizing that the ox team was about done. The beasts had dragged the heavy weight up some bad grades where footing had been miserable and it was clear that they could not go much farther.

The need for decision was taken out of his hands. They came up behind the waiting ambulance and found that Mellew had gotten himself into heavy timber with no apparent way around it.

Hale took a quick survey, groping rather than looking. "Ground starts to drop off ahead," he told them when he came back. "No point in risking it. We'll stay right here and wait for daylight. Get comfortable—if you can."

"What about the outlaws?" Garnsey asked nervously.

"Don't worry about them. Sooner or later they'll catch up with us—and we'll see who they think is their friend in this crew. But don't expect it to happen for a few days. Nobody's going to come across the Red for a while—unless he can sprout wings."

"Want us to unhitch now?" Jakes called to him.

"No. We'd only have extra confusion. The animals will have to stick it out just as they stand—and that goes for the rest of us. Don't any of you try to change to dry clothes they'd only get wet as soon as you put them on. If you've got anything dry try to keep it that way for later."

"Ain't a damned thing dry nowhere," Tolliver growled.

"We'd be just as wet on the south bank," Jakes told him with a short laugh. "And in a lot more trouble. Me, I'll stay wet over here and like it."

Hale dismounted, again tying his horse to a wheel of the big wagon. Then he climbed up to where Shattuck had huddled silently on the driver's seat. "How's Susie?" he asked.

The old man practically snapped at him. "I dunno. Gittin' so nobody tells me nothin'. Nothin' about her, that is."

"Try being decent to her," Hale said in a low tone. "It might help."

He poked his head through a canvas flap and asked, "Susie awake yet?"

"Ah wish Ah wasn't," the girl answered for herself. "Ah ain't nevah felt so mizzuble in mah life. Why in hell didn't yo' let me drown peaceful like?"

"You must be doing fine," he told her with a laugh. "Anybody has got to be pretty healthy to bellyache like that. How's the wound?"

"Ah dunno. Ah could be bleedin' to death and Ah wouldn't know blood from wateh!"

Betsy interrupted, "Maybe you can tell the difference in the dark. She's right. We can't tell whether the wound is open or not."

Hale eased himself back across the wagon's seat and found a hand reaching out to meet him. There were rings on the hand so he knew that it was Betsy's.

"Easy does it," the blonde warned. "I've got the water out of her so it won't help any for you to try squeezing more out."

"What do you expect of me?" he snapped.

"Just what I said. Maybe you can tell blood from water in the dark. I can't see a damned thing but I need to know. Unless the wound is open I don't want to try fooling with that bandage at a time like this. I might do more harm than good."

Another hand came out then and Susie said, "Ah'm oveh on this side. Let me show yo'."

She drew his hand down, Betsy releasing her hold, and he could feel sodden cloth under his fingers. Susie didn't take her hand away and he wasn't sure why. Maybe she was making certain that his fingers didn't move into other areas or maybe she had some other idea.

Betsy must have been reading a part of his thought for she said quietly, "Just feel the compress, mister. Nothing else." It seemed as though the words were not too serious.

"I think it's mostly water," he told them without making any attempt to acknowledge the implied warning. "Blood would be more slippery."

"Then the wound hasn't opened?"

"I don't think so—and I'm a bit surprised. We had to handle her a mite rough."

"Thanks—for ever'thing, Cap'n," Susie told him in a low tone. "Ah didn't have no call to git mean-mouthed a couple o' minutes ago. It was mighty decent of yo' to haul me outa that riveh."

"Forget it. Just get yourself as much rest as you can. We'll be moving as soon as there's light and the next haul could get pretty rocky. You'll need all the grit you can muster."

He was groping for the wagon seat as he spoke. There were a lot of things more important that he needed to think about. Puzzling over a couple of women was something that he could omit.

Chapter 13

Somehow the wet, miserable night passed. Hale even managed to catch a few winks of sleep in the mud under the Shattuck wagon. When he woke up cold he crawled out into the rain again, prowling around to make certain that things hadn't gotten into any new mess since the halt. The teams and the extra stock had stamped about until they were deep in slippery mud but otherwise nothing seemed to be amiss. Compared to the situation which had faced the little company only half a day earlier this was wonderful.

When the first streaks of gray began to show through thinning clouds he routed his companions out and gave them fresh instructions. That was what they now expected of him so that was what they were going to get. He had stopped being conscious of any change in himself. He could almost forget that there had been months when he had refused to accept any kind of responsibility. Now there was a job facing him. Several jobs, really. He thought only of seeing things through.

"Rain's about over, folks," he told them with a show of cheerfulness. "We'll move as soon as we can see our way. No time to fool around with a fire, even if we could get one started. Break out whatever hard rations you've got and save your appetites for later. Time won't be too big a problem today so don't worry about meals. Ben, what do you remember about this stretch of country?"

"Damn little. It's kinda like the other side only there's better grass behind this ridge."

"Did we cross any creeks that'll be too high for wagons?"

"I don't remember none."

"Let's try to stick with the ridge as long as we can. Less mud up here so the big problem will be to find a trail through the timber. You start scouting for an opening as soon as you've got something in your belly. We'll wait for you to tell us which way the wagons are going to have to go. Jakes will act as train leader and keep in touch with you. Keep the ambulance in front but be ready to lend a hand if the big wagon gets stuck."

He went into further details while they were eating. Then Old Ben rode away into the clearing morning. The rain had definitely passed and there were even bits of blue sky beginning to show.

Hale put his saddle on one of the extra horses, having first looked in to make sure that Susie was all right. The girl was sound asleep but Betsy affirmed his guess of the night. The wound had not opened.

He eased down the slippery grade to the lower patches of timber. Within a few minutes he could see enough water through the trees to know that the Red was in full flood. He guessed that there must be a good six feet of water covering the spot where the wagons had first halted after coming out of the ford. The rapid rise of the river had cost them a wagon and a team but it had given them far more. There would be no pursuit for some days.

He circled back toward the creek which had the sandbar at its mouth, discovering that the smaller stream was not as swollen as the river. The Red actually seemed to be backing some of its yellow flood into the tributary so he knew that the heavier fall of water had been somewhere to the west. That was good because it meant that the high water in the river would continue for a little longer than he had first hoped.

His new vantage point gave him a good view of the swollen river below the creek junction and he stared with interest at the way the yellow expanse had changed the appearance of the entire valley. No longer was there a channel with mudflats and a stretch of bottomlands. Now the cottonwoods appeared to be mere bushes in mid-river. The water was well up on the slope where the ambush had been attempted. Where the wagons had halted for their long wait seemed to be just another part of the river.

Suddenly he realized that someone was moving about along the far shore some three quarters of a mile downstream. His first impression was that a party of travelers had come along just in time to get into a lot of trouble, but then he had a better look and saw that one of the men at the water's edge was notably large. Maddigan and some of his gang must have made an early move in hopes of catching their expected quarry storm-bound. Now they were heading on down the river believing that they were on the trail of retreating wagons. What they were doing at the river's edge Hale couldn't quite make out.

He moved to a slightly higher spot and found that his angle of vision was improved. The distance was still too great for him to see details but he felt sure that the men down-river were trying to haul something out of the flood. Evidently they had put a rope on the object and were working it in toward solid ground. When a man brought up a couple of horses Hale knew that he had guessed correctly.

After some delay he got a good look at what was in the edge of the river. Only a little of it showed but it seemed like a safe bet that he was looking at the Garnsey wagon. A quirk of the current had thrown it against brush so that it had not gone downstream very far. Probably the dead horses had further tangled it so that it had lodged against something.

But why were the outlaws so interested? Did they need an extra wagon for distribution of the stolen muskets? They were going to a lot of trouble to get this particular ambulance.

His vigil turned out to be a rather lengthy one. He saw other men ride east to join the men he had first spotted. Other horses were put to work. Finally the wagon came out, the drowned horses having apparently been cut loose.

What happened next didn't seem to make any sense at all. They were tearing the wagon apart. Details were still impossible but he knew that at least two wheels had been pitched into the roaring river. It seemed like a peculiar kind of diversion for men who certainly had other things to do.

He studied their moves until they mounted and rode back toward him. Then he swung to hurry after his own party. Only one explanation made any sense but that one told him plenty. He didn't propose to talk about it, but he definitely had to keep it in mind.

The wagons, when he overtook them, were on the soggy prairie north of the ridge, making slow progress. The higher ground had been bad enough but on the lower level the footing was even worse. Mellew's mules still pulled with some show of strength but Shattuck's oxen were about worn out.

Hale quickly called a halt. "We'll kill the stock if we try to force the pace any longer," he told Jakes. "For a day or so, at least, we don't have to worry about Maddigan's crowd. We'll do ourselves a good turn if we take time to rest ourselves and the animals. No point in being all worn to a frazzle before the real crisis happens. Set up camp in those trees just ahead. I'll ride on and see if I can find Ben. Then we'll look the country over a bit. Maddigan may not be the only enemy around here."

There was a quick protest at the order, but Hale had expected it. Retreat was something that few people could handle without losing their poise. These folks were like soldiers who were ordered to pull back in the face of the enemy. It would take careful handling to keep an orderly retreat from becoming something like panic.

"Figure it this way," Hale said quietly when both Mellew and Garnsey had tried to argue in favor of continued travel. "These flash floods taper off almost as fast as they rise. Perhaps in a day or two Maddigan and his men will be able to cross the river. If they're smart and know the country they'll go up along the south bank to cross at a different ford. That puts them close on our heels no matter what we do."

"So what did we gain by crossing?" Garnsey snapped. "I lost a wagon and a damned fine pair of horses!"

"But you've still got a whole skin—which likely you wouldn't have if we'd stayed on the other side. Our move was one of delay. Nobody claimed it would get us clean away."

"Stop squalling!" Jakes told the little man. "We got out of a bad spot and now we've got chances.

We didn't have any back there. Shut your fat mouth and do what the man tells you to do!"

"It's this way," Hale went on, trying to avoid any quarrel in the party. "Today we're ruining our teams and not making good progress. By waiting a half day we'll give the mud a chance to settle. We'll all be rested and we'll more than make up the lost time on good ground. It's simply common sense."

Susie's voice sounded from the big wagon. "Do what he tell yo'! He ain't been wrong yet."

Hale grinned. "You heard the lady," he said solemnly. Then he rode away, having talked as much as he intended to. It made him wonder a little that he should be depending on Jakes to carry out his orders, but he was beginning to think that he understood the lean man's motives. Jakes would do all right on the present job.

When he caught up with Old Ben he told him only that the outlaws were searching the south bank and that they had found Garnsey's ambulance. "They won't be long in heading up-river," he said. "If they knew the area well enough to send the gun wagons to a hiding place it's a cinch they know it well enough to know about the upper ford."

They made a wide circle but saw no sign of life anywhere along the north side of the Red. When they rode back to the new camp Betsy Appleby was the only one not sound asleep. She was working at a cooking fire that had been built in the open away from the wagons and her first word was one of complaint about wet wood.

"I'll git ye some dead stuff," Tolliver volunteered. "Dead-on-the-stump kind is what ye need. It'll be drier and it'll ketch hold faster. Deader it is the better." He looked sideways at Hale before he added, "Like ole Ben Franklin useta say, 'There ain't no fuel like a old fuel.' I reckon he had the right idee."

"Don't let on that you even heard him," Hale advised solemnly. "No point in encouraging him. He's bad enough as he is. What's cooking?"

"Stew. And it's about ready. Want some?"

"Sure. You're getting to be quite a cook."

She brushed back a string of still damp hair and grimaced. "Never expected it, did you?"

"I don't know. Seems like a lot of people turned out better than I expected them to. Last night, I mean."

"And now they're sleepin' with full bellies, pretendin' that they're not the worms they really are! Better do your own filling up and sleeping. In no time at all you're going to have to start knocking heads. When the scare's over they'll be ornery as ever."

"Thanks for the advice. I'll try to keep it in mind. I'll be looking to make sure that you don't try to talk Susie into joining you."

She looked embarrassed but met his stare

quickly. "Sorry I talked that way to her. I could use her, I'm sure, but I'm not going to start any fight with you over her."

Hale nodded. "That's settled. Now what else do I need to look out for? From the others, I mean."

"I'm not the one to say. I just have a feeling about it."

"Any real idea why everybody's out to catch Mellew, for example?"

"I don't know any more than you do. I heard the same stories. I think they want the gold Mellew's supposed to have. It wouldn't make any difference to either of them that he hasn't got it. They still think he has."

"What do you think? Does he?"

"I've already told you my story. It was the true one. I didn't know Mellew and he didn't know me. I didn't have any hint about gold until the other day across the river. After that I made my own search of the wagon. I'll swear that there's no false bottom in it or any of that kind of trick. Somebody just got the story messed up."

"But Maddigan would be just as determined to get Mellew because he still thinks the gold is there. Is that the idea?"

She nodded. "That's the idea. Gold fever is a bad disease. Believe me, I know. I think you were right when you said Maddigan probably hid those guns while he went looking for plunder."

"There's still another angle. Maybe he was in on

some kind of a deal with Garnsey. He wants cartridges."

"Could be. Most crooks are mighty greedy." Somehow it was easy to forget who she was when she talked like that.

Tolliver came in then with an armload of dead wood so Hale finished his stew in silence and found a place in the sun where he could stretch out. His clothing was already pretty well dried out so he didn't concern himself about it. The main thing was to let tired eyes fall shut for a while.

When he became conscious again it was to a lazy sort of knowledge that all was well around him. The sun was low in the west and a murmur of talk let him know that the others had taken their rest and were up again. The snatches of conversation that penetrated his sleepiness told him that they were getting back to what passed for normal with this group. They were arguing.

"Sure oxen is slow," Shattuck's voice came. "But they hold up good. And they're safer fer Injun country. Injuns will steal hosses any time they can git 'em. They like mule meat so they'll steal mules. But they figger as how any kind of cow is just poor grade buffalo and they don't bother."

Mellew jeered. "Who told you a fool thing like that? Injuns like beef all right. Mules kinda worry 'em 'cause they don't understand the critters. That's how an old-timer told it to me, so I got mules."

Shattuck laughed loudly. "Musta been some old-timer what had mules to sell. Likely thought he was real smart playin' tricks on a greenhorn sailor."

Hale didn't hear the rest of the argument. When he woke up again the talk was louder and a little more serious. This time it was Jakes and Garnsey and the subject was secession. "Sure I went along with it," Jakes was saying. "I had to. You rabble-rousers didn't give anybody a chance to talk sense. You called Sam Houston a traitor when he tried to make you see what fools you were making of yourselves. Anybody who didn't want to get crucified by you either joined up or kept quiet."

"But secession was our legal right!" Garnsey shouted.

"In Texas—yes. We joined the Union of our own free will, just like the original thirteen states did. I think any of that lot—or us—had a good legal right to pull out if we wanted to. But it's nonsense to claim that Florida and Louisiana had any such right. They were bought and paid for by the Union. They didn't join up as free units. They were in before anybody let them become states. Just property of the others, you might say. For them to claim a right of secession was damned bad law and worse logic."

"Have it your own way, lawyer! I was talking about Texas. We had a right to secede!"

"A right. Sure. I agreed on that already. What

I'm saying is that it didn't make sense. I've got a right to cut off my hand if I want to but it don't make much sense to do it. Texas didn't have a thing to gain by going along with those South Carolina catfish aristocrats."

"We had ties with the South."

"Damned few. Not enough to get killed over—and that's what your damned foolishness did. Our best men gone—and now you're trying to get more killing started!"

"Now you're making up a dastardly claim!"

"You know it's the truth, you crazy fool! Can't you get it through your weasel mind that the Yanks will knock hell out of us if they catch us stirring up an Indian war? And don't say you weren't planning it. I know the truth! You had it all fixed to meet that gunrunner bandit and deliver guns and cartridges together."

Hale was listening with all his faculties by that time but it didn't do much good. Garnsey admitted nothing, simply getting up and leaving the fire where the talk had been going on. So Hale went back to sleep again.

Some time later he heard Shattuck relating how he had gathered some trade goods together and had worked out what he thought would be a safe route to the Indian country. His idea had been to hit the Red far enough upstream to avoid the Union patrols that had become active close to the Louisiana line, actually picking much the same trail that the peace party had used. He was a little bitter about the miscalculation. Nobody had told him about the risk of running into bandits, gun-runners, gold smugglers, renegades, and various other kinds of rats who were leaving the sinking ship of the Confederacy.

Suddenly it was dark. Hale knew that he had slept again and that somebody was trying to shake him awake. "Trouble?" he asked quickly.

"Hadn't oughta be none," Susie told him. "Ah figgahed as how yo' might want to git some sentries out."

"What are you doing out of your bunk?"

"Movin' around real spry. So don't gimme no sass. Ah'm about done with bein' a invalid."

In the dim light from the fire he could see that she was dressed as she had been when he had first seen her. Only the floppy hat was missing.

"No sentries," he told her, sitting up. "We won't need any tonight, I feel sure. So get back to your blankets and take care of that wound. I may need you real bad before long."

"Yo're jest talkin' that way to josh me along."

"Hold it! Remember that you don't have to be snappish with me just because you're sore about the way Uncle Golly talks to you."

"But yo' try to baby me—almost as much as he's doin'."

"I'm just using good sense—and you know it."

"One thing Ah'm rememberin' is that yo' pulled

me outa the rivah. Seems like Ah owe yo' some-thin' fer that."

"Likely you'll get a chance to even it up—if you're fit and able. So get back to the wagon. That's an order."

She hesitated but then uttered a little laugh. "Yes, suh, Cap'n," she agreed formally. "Ah'm a-goin'."

He wasn't quite sure why she had found it funny.

Chapter 14

He sat by the dying fire for several minutes, sipping strong coffee and trying to make himself believe that he wasn't as stiff and sore as he really was. The others had gone back to sleep again, still not caught up on their rest after the stormy ordeal. A first quarter moon let him see that work had been done around the camp and he wondered who had done the necessary prodding to get it done. He could still feel a mild amazement at the way these people had performed under pressure. But that was the way it often turned out to be in the army; some times the worst soldiers at drill were the best fighters.

He checked axles for grease, harness for weaknesses, the stock for possible injuries. Everywhere he found indications of recent care. Finally he was satisfied that the outfit was ready for the big haul so he went back to the fire and sat near the glowing embers, glad to be there as the night's chill made itself felt.

He wondered why he didn't get away from this crowd now that they were showing so much ability to take care of themselves. His only duty now was to locate the wagons that he felt must contain the stolen muskets. At least he had a duty to find out if there were guns in them. He had no obligation to people who might prove to be his enemies in a crisis.

Then he realized that he was making mental excuses for staying. His argument to his inner mind was good enough, the point that the other wagon tracks would now be washed away and there would be no easy way to locate the gun runners. By remaining with a party that Maddigan intended to chase he would be more certain to keep an eye on men who would eventually lead him to the contraband weapons. It was a good argument but he knew that it wasn't the real reason he didn't ride out and go looking for the guns.

He spent a little more time trying to guess how various members of his party would react if it came to a showdown fight but gave up on the problem. The harsh fact was that he couldn't really trust any of them. So far they had done better than he could have expected, but the future might work out differently. It was one of the worst features of the whole prospect.

When he went back to the tarp he had used for bedding he found a dry blanket with it. He'd seen no one near it so he wondered who had left it. Oddly enough, he told himself, it might have been a gesture by either Susie or Betsy. Which was another problem, one he didn't even want to think about.

The whole camp was stirring long before

daylight, sleep drained out of them after the long halt. Hale explained his plan of operation and didn't hear a single objection. The line of march would be just as it had been earlier, Tolliver working out a trail and Jakes serving as train leader. When the ponies had been captured after the ambush fight there had been only one saddle found, both of the Indians and the Negro having dispensed with such gear. Now Jakes was to take over Lorry Ryan's outfit and leave Susie's gear for the girl's own use in the event of an emergency. For today she was to stay in her uncle's wagon, lying down as much as possible. Susie was the only one who even started to put up a protest at the marching orders.

"We'll move out as soon as you're ready," Hale told them. "I'm going back to keep an eye on the river. I'll want to know where the outlaws plan to cross and it'll be important to us to know how soon they can manage it."

"Jest like ole Moses," Tolliver cackled. "He brung the Israelites across the Red Sea with the 'Gyptians hard on their tails. Now this crowd's come across the Red River but the Maddiganites is chasin' us. Pharaoh's army didn't git drownded."

Hale made a wry face at Ben and rode away. The Tolliver style of philosophy seemed to be getting worse every day.

He swung to a line that was roughly parallel to the one the wagons were taking, holding to the top of the ridge until it was light enough for him to see the river. Everything seemed to be as completely flooded as it had been a day earlier. That was fine. He could only hope that the water would stay up for another three days or more. By that time his party would have swung away from the Red and be headed toward the Washita. Until that much time could pass they would not actually be putting much distance between themselves and the outlaws.

While he scanned the country he tried to figure on battle plans. Sooner or later they would be overtaken. Probably Maddigan would try to hit them along the trail to Washita, but it was also likely that the big thug would be pressed for time. A direct attack from the rear would be the most likely prospect so Hale tried to think of some way to handle it.

Just thinking about the possibilities was a disturbing business. The actual number of enemies was not as bad as the discouraging odds in the matter of weapons. Maddigan's men were evidently supplied with muskets as well as any other arms they might have carried. To meet their attack the wagoners were in pitiful shape. Hale and Tolliver both had six-guns but Old Ben had not located much of a supply of ammunition for the revolver he'd taken from Ryan's body. He would have to depend a lot on the carbine. Jakes had lost his dragoon pistols when the Garnsey wagon went down the Red. Only Mellew's musket and Susie's carbine rounded out the defense armament. There were not enough guns in the outfit to meet half the attack that could be expected.

They made a good day of it until just after mid-afternoon. Then Hale heard a gun shot. He abandoned his scouting job and sent his horse at a gallop through the screening timber to where the wagons had halted on the edge of lush prairie. Tolliver came hammering back at the same time, both men with weapons in their hands as they looked for the expected enemy.

Jakes explained what had happened, apologetic at the false alarm. The wagons had been crossing a harmless looking little gully when one of the mules had slipped on a rock not big enough to seem dangerous. The animal had broken a leg and had been shot.

"What now?" Jakes asked. "Can we get along with a team of one horse and one mule?"

"Better to use Garnsey's spare grays," Hale told him. "Turn the other mule loose; he'll be more trouble to take along than he'll be worth. From here on we've got to move fast."

Both Garnsey and Mellew wanted to argue but Hale shouted them down. "We've got to make the turn north as soon as we can," he told them. "Not until then do we really begin to gain on Maddigan. Change those teams in a hurry and get going. It's no time to worry over whose property is getting the brunt of the trouble. We use what we can."

Garnsey was still grumbling over the loss of his wagon and horses when they made camp that night. The others seemed pleased over the obvious fact that they'd made up the distance that had been lost by resting, but Garnsey seemed to feel that he was getting all the bad breaks. At supper Jakes began to prod him pretty hard, telling him that he wasn't getting any worse luck than he deserved.

"It was a damned fool thing for you to put money into any kind of outfit for this trip in the first place. I don't mean just the part about how much of an idiot you had to be over stirrin' up Indians; I mean the part about thinkin' the war could be stretched out. You've been admittin' all along that we were licked."

"I never admitted anything of the sort!" Garnsey snarled. "I still don't think so." Obviously he preferred to keep the talk on something other than the suspected Indian plot. "And don't tell anybody I ever said we'd lose!"

"Your actions said so."

"What actions, damn you?"

"Calm down. That's the trouble with idiots like you. As soon as anybody starts to talk sense you're licked. With no argument to offer you start to cuss. How long has it been since you'd take Confederate notes for any kind of debt? How long has it been since you've found a shop-keeper who'd accept them for merchandise?"

"What's that got to do with it?"

"Everything. Confederate paper was going at a big discount even before Gettysburg and Vicksburg. Why? Because everybody knew it would never be redeemed. A government issues paper money, promisin' to redeem it in hard cash at some future time. If the government is in good shape the promise will be kept. If the government is likely to fail nobody wants their notes because there's no chance that they'll ever be redeemed."

"Now you're talking a lot of damned nonsense!"

"You know better. There's nothing in the world that people are more practical about than money. Two years ago people started balkin' at Confederate paper. No matter what they said in words they were sayin' in their business dealin's that they expected the Confederacy to welsh on its obligations. They were predictin' that it would fail as a government and default as a debtor. You said it every time you argued over takin' a Confederate note. I'll bet you've even used Yankee greenbacks when you could get them. When you did that you were really saying that you expected the Union to win and to pay off."

Tolliver broke in then. "Ole Ben Franklin had a sayin' about 'actions speak louder'n words.' Mebbe he meant somethin' like what ye're sayin' now."

Hale wandered away. He had a feeling that Jakes was up to something with this heckling campaign but he couldn't quite decide what it meant. There didn't seem to be any great reason to prod Garnsey now. The man's schemes were pretty well shattered. Likely enough Jakes was simply trying to establish his own position in the eyes of someone else, using Garnsey as a foil. Somehow it didn't sound like the whole explanation. Jakes must have something else on his mind. He had lied about the Mellew affair right at the start.

They moved out again before dawn, lined up as before but with Jakes doing the trail scouting. Tolliver was to push on ahead and look for signs of those gun wagons. With Maddigan and most of his men still on the south side of the Red there was a chance to make a strike at the wagons before the outlaws could get back to defend them. Hale had to do anything possible along that line. If the river would stay flooded for another couple of days he had a chance.

He rode the high ground again, but for a couple of hours the mists kept him from seeing much of the valley. Then he saw that the water was subsiding at an alarming rate. If it continued to fall the way it had done during the night the wagon party would be in trouble. Maddigan would reach the upper ford and make the crossing before the fugitives could get far away from the river.

An hour later he knew that Maddigan was continuing to show familiarity with the country.

He had not wasted time along the lower river but was pressing on upstream in an effort to ride around the sweep of the flood. Hale got a good look at the whole gang, the bulk of Maddigan himself making identification simple even at the distance.

Now that there seemed to be no chance of any immediate move against the hidden gun wagons he made a quick decision. The country was strange to him but he knew that the trail from the Red to the Washita could not be far ahead. Memory told him that it ran across rolling prairie with no particular difficulties at this stretch. There seemed to be no good reason why the wagons should not angle across and try to save time with a shortcut. Maybe the outlaws would waste time in picking up the trail on the north side. And maybe the gun wagons had taken a similar short-cut. Somebody in Maddigan's outfit seemed to know this country pretty well so such a device might have been used.

He wasted no time when he rode back to the little train. "We'll swing to the northwest as soon as we cross that next little creek. We'll have to go it blind for a while but the country looks good and there won't be any water problem for a week or so. By that time we'll be through it or . . ."

"Why leave the river?" Jakes asked. He had ridden back to the wagons at sight of Hale's return.

Hale explained. "We could gain quite a bit if Maddigan wastes time looking for our sign near the ford."

Jakes grinned. "Lead on, Moses. But don't plan to spend any forty years in the wilderness."

The laugh that followed helped to ease any doubts that the others might have had and the wagons moved out across the prairie. There had been no trail up the river so it didn't make any particular difference.

It was night before Old Ben found them on the unplanned trail and his report was one of failure. There had been no wagons, no sign, no indication of a camp. Hale began to hope that his guess had been correct, that the guns were somewhere ahead on the trail to Washita.

They passed the night along a clear creek and somehow the tension seemed to have eased. Jakes didn't stir up any new arguments with Garnsey. Mellew had turned silent, but that was not surprising. Everyone was tired enough so that all they wanted to do was to get some supper and fall asleep. Hale rode a complete circle around the camp just before sundown and found no indication that anyone had been near the place for days. Accordingly he did not set up any watches; he and Tolliver would be up early enough to do some scouting before daybreak.

The night passed without alarm and they moved on again in the first grays of dawn, Hale letting the others get started before he cut back toward the river, promising to overtake them before noon.

His scouting trip didn't please him too well. Almost immediately he realized that he had been wrong in his estimate of the distance of the ford. As soon as he mounted the high country near the river he saw some of the landmarks that he had seen on the trip west with the peace commission. The shortcut hadn't saved much distance—and the river was still dropping at a rapid rate.

He didn't waste time looking for Maddigan and his crowd. It was clear that they would soon be coming across the river so he simply headed north. He picked up his party's tracks in mid-morning, getting some small satisfaction out of the fact that they were making good progress on a course that was angling in on the regular trail.

Minutes later he saw a rider directly ahead of him and started to look for cover, thinking that perhaps one of the gun wagon guards might have moved in behind the fugitives. Then he realized that the rider was Susie. Apparently she had taken advantage of his absence to get back into action.

She pulled aside to wait for him and he noted that she was wearing her regular scout garb but had again omitted the battered hat. The wind had blown her close-cropped hair into disorder but it still looked pretty good—and he had a feeling that she knew it.

"Time Ah got back on the job," she greeted, her

smile suggesting that she hoped he wouldn't give her any argument on that subject.

He nodded, matching her smile. "I suppose you'll do as you please so I won't say what I was going to. Now stop trying to sit up straight. I know that you're just trying to convince me that you're all well again."

"Don't git so smart," she complained, the smile still on. "Ah didn't figger yo'd notice."

He didn't tell her that he could have scarcely failed to notice. When she sat up like that the bandages put just a little extra into the notable fullness of her shirt-front. "River's going down fast," he told her, electing to stay with a safer subject. "Maddigan won't be long in getting over to this side. I'm going to need plenty of help from the folks I can trust."

"Still includin' me in yore list?"

"Don't start being coy!"

"What's that mean?"

"Maybe you don't know the word but you've got the idea."

She frowned a little but then smiled again. "Ah dunno why but Ah kinda like the way yo' say that."

Chapter 15

Hale changed the subject. "Are you sure you can sit in the saddle for a while without it getting painful to you?"

She still refused to be serious. "This saddle ain't pressin' none on no tender spot."

"Stop trying to be shocking. I'm not your uncle."

"What do yo' mean by that?"

"You know. You're sore at the way he keeps trying to treat you like a little kid so you do everything you can think of to worry him. Don't try it on me. I've got other things to think about. Can you handle this rear guard job for the rest of the day?"

"Ah reckon so. What's got yo' itchin' so bad that yo've got to be somewhere else? Me?"

"Listen carefully and stop the nonsense. We'll have that gang behind us pretty soon and I want to know it as soon as they show up. Meanwhile I want to ride ahead and make sure that Ben don't miss the regular trail. It's no more than an Indian path and he might cut right on past because he won't be expecting to hit it so soon."

Her nod was serious enough but then she shook her head with a show of chagrin. "Yo' mean yo'd rather ride with him than with me?"

"I told you to stop being silly. We're in trouble."

She continued with her act. "Well, every feller to his own taste, as the old woman said when she kissed the cow. Git on up there."

"Holy Smoke! Now you're sounding like Old Ben."

"If that's yore choice o' comp'ny Ah thought Ah'd give it to yo'."

This time he had to smile at her show of humor. "If you talk like that to your uncle it's no wonder he worries about you."

"He worries about ever'thing. Soon as Ah stahted bein' halfway growed up he stahted worryin'. Seemed like Ah might as well help him along, bein' as how he'd imagine things to worry about if'n Ah didn't give him some. He near busted his suspenders when Ah tole him Ah was thinkin' about goin' along with Belle if'n we got outa this mess."

"With Belle! Are you crazy?"

"She ast me."

"Stay clear of her! I don't wonder Uncle Golly thinks you're a bad lot. You go out of your way to make yourself look bad."

"Ah didn't ask fer yore advice." She tried to make it sound dignified but didn't quite manage it.

"I'm giving it to you. Any monkey business with Belle and I'll help your uncle wallop you."

"That's real nice," she told him with the smile

coming back. "Ah was hopin' yo'd talk that way about it."

He stared for a moment, reading the satisfaction in her brown eyes, then he turned and headed up the trail. There wasn't much point in making any new remarks. He was only getting himself into deeper troubles with every word.

He went past the wagons, telling them of the new arrangements, and hurried on to overtake Tolliver. Almost as soon as he fell in beside Old Ben they struck the trail that Hale had covered with the Commissioner. It was only an Indian path but it followed terrain that the wagons could negotiate easily—and it led directly to the spot where the peace talks must still be going on. With a bit of luck the wagoners might hope to meet enough other people so that Maddigan would hesitate to attack. It wasn't a good bet that anything like that would happen but it was better than no chance at all.

They didn't halt for the night until darkness was almost upon them. The hours of relaxation were gone and everyone moved in tense silence as camp chores were performed. Hale was content to have it that way. He wanted them getting every bit of rest possible. Another day might find all of them drawing on every bit of surplus energy available.

They moved out before dawn, Hale setting up a new marching order only when daylight began to show. Tolliver was to continue in the lead with Jakes remaining close to the wagons. Hale would act as rear guard, on the lookout for the first signs of pursuit. Susie would hold a position halfway between Hale and the wagons, ready to relay the word for the wagoners to get ready for defense. It would come to that, of course. None of them were doubting it now.

Late in the morning Hale decided that he hadn't planned too well so he rode forward and told Susie to hold her position for a few minutes so that they would be changing places. "Don't take any chances," he warned. "As soon as you see anybody on the back trail get right up here and pass the word. I think they'll catch up with us pretty soon now; they'll be riding plenty fast."

"Worryin' about me?" she inquired with another of those elfin grins.

"Yes, damn it. Now stick to business!"

His next move was to have Jakes and Mellew trade places. Jakes would handle the team, not being needed in the lead now that the wagons were following a well-defined trail. "I want you to stick with me," he told Mellew. "Everything that's happened so far suggests that it's you Maddigan wants. Maybe it's for what you've got, or maybe it's for something they think you've got. To us it don't make a bit of difference. The point is that the danger points in your direction so I thought maybe we might hold them up for some kind of a confab if they could see you. We won't take wild chances, of course, but maybe it could keep us out of a general battle."

"They won't believe me when I tell 'em I haven't got any gold," Mellew growled, "but it's worth a try. Where do we ride?"

"I don't need Jakes," Betsy called from the wagon. "I can handle a team. Let him stay out ahead; it might help."

Hale nodded his agreement. "Come on, Mellew. We'll relieve Susie as the rear guard."

The stocky man laughed as though he had no personal problems in the matter. "Maybe we should leave her back there. A gal with her build has got a lot more chance of stoppin' Maddigan than I'll have."

A horse for Mellew suddenly became a problem and Jakes had to take the wagon after all. Hale wondered why Betsy had tried to keep him away but he didn't propose to think about little matters like that now. He simply waited until Mellew was in the saddle Jakes had just vacated and then they were easing back to relieve Susie and put her in the relay position again. Hale offered one additional bit of advice. "Better join up with Tolliver if we have to go into a defense position. He's a good man in a tight spot."

Less than twenty minutes after the shift of positions they spotted riders on the back trail. Maddigan had made the crossing without much delay—and he had not been fooled by the lack of wagon tracks along the river. Now he was coming up along the Indian trail at a pace which reminded Hale of his earlier hunch that somebody in the Maddigan outfit knew the country pretty well.

"Keep an eye on 'em," Hale said briefly. "Try to ride so that they don't shorten the distance on you. I'll be back with you before they get close."

"What's on your mind now?"

"A hunch about where to halt the wagons." He was riding away as he spoke, looking over his shoulder to see that Mellew was keeping the same pace as before. When he passed Susie she called out, "How come no signal? Don't yo' trust me no moah?"

He pulled up suddenly and swung back to her. "Sure I trust you. So you go ahead and tell Ben what I was going to tell him. I seem to remember a deep but narrow ravine somewhere along this part of the trail. Tell Ben to be on the lookout for it. Tell him the gang is coming up behind us so we'll have to find some place to make a stand. The creek would be a good bet if we can reach it. I'm not sure we can. Tell him to pick a good spot within the next hour. If we don't find the creek some other place will have to do. Got it?"

"Ah got it. What do Ah do afteh that?"

"Stay with the wagons. Take your orders from Sergeant Tolliver. Side him if it comes to a fight."

"What was yo' expectin' to be doin' all this time?"

"Hard to tell. You know what we're going to try. I think you won't be long in finding out how we succeed. Don't wait for me. Just do what I've told you."

She started to turn her horse but then hesitated before saying, "One thing, Cap'n. Ah ain't much at nice talk but Ah want to thank yo' fer pullin' me outa that wagon. In case we don't git outa this—it was mighty damn . . . I mean mighty nice meetin' yo'."

It was amazing how different she could sound when she tried. And she had been trying, sure enough, even to the point of catching herself in a swear-word. The second time she'd done it, he recalled.

He waited for Mellew to reach him, noting that the pursuing riders had closed the distance slightly. Now he could count them. There were eight of them. The number bothered him for a few moments but then he decided that he could account for the eighth man—Jed, of course, being the seventh. The gun wagons had not taken a shortcut but were hidden somewhere along the river, probably close to the upper ford. One of the drivers had been picked up by the band for added strength.

"You let them gain on you," he told Mellew.

"Not much. I figured it'd be good to let them see

me. Might slow 'em down a bit if they got to wonderin'."

Hale shrugged. "Could be. Let's ride."

An hour later there could be no question as to the identity of the eight. Twice Hale had caught them in the open where individuals loomed against flat background. Maddigan's bulk could be picked out easily enough. Once he was sure about it he let them gain a little more rapidly. The interval between the rear guard and the wagons had to be maintained as long as possible.

"You ain't plannin' to meet 'em right out in the open, are you?" Mellew asked nervously when the outlaws were only a mile in the rear. "Don't figure they'll pay any attention to that flag-of-truce stuff. They'll kill if they get a chance, no matter what."

"We'll find cover before we try anything," Hale promised.

Another forty minutes saw the eight riders well within the half mile. At that point Susie hurried back along the wagon tracks to announce that they had found the creek Hale had described.

"We figgah as how theah's a purty good place to make a stand," she told Hale excitedly. "Ben's gittin' the wagons across. We'll . . ."

"Hold it! You make it sound as though you've got the whole thing all planned."

She made a face at him and he found himself grinning in return. Her excitement was infectious.

"Yo' needn't think yo're the only one with brains around heah," she told him loftily. "Ben and me figgahed it out real good. The wagons go outa sight behind a couple o' little hills west o' the crick. We'all use the crick fer trenches. It's easy."

Hale nodded toward Mellew. "Let's take a look and see what kind of strategists Generals Ben and Susie are. Maybe the creek will be the point where we can try some kind of confab."

They galloped ahead, crossing a piece of higher ground that let them glance back at the pursuers. It would also give the outlaws a look at three riders and might make them grow a bit cautious. That was what Hale wanted; cautious men might be a little more ready for a parley.

When they reached the creek crossing, the wagons were already out of sight. Hale could see the tactical value of the location but he could also see a glaring weakness. The creek wasn't wide but it was deep, practically a gulley and already nearly dry as the flood waters drained away. Wagons could cross it only at the point where the trail showed, but riders could make the crossing at almost any place. The regular crossing could be defended, but it could be flanked quite simply.

"Better than the open," he told Susie. "Mellew and I will stay right here and try to talk with Maddigan. You ride on and tell Ben what we're planning to try. Have him bring Jakes along so that the two of them can support us from those bushes on the hill. Your job will be to defend the wagons if any of the gang gets past us."

"Why not give them a dose of their own medicine?" Mellew growled. "They wanted to ambush us. Let's do the same for 'em. Get Jakes and the others here into the crick with us. With the wagons outa sight we could knock hell out of 'em before they knew we was even around."

"No. I'm still a lawman, you know. We'll stay under cover while we try talk—but we'll still try talk!"

"You're a damned fool. They wouldn't give us no chance."

"We'll have to try. Pick yourself a good spot in the gulley and make sure that your musket is ready for business. Have your extra cartridges and caps where you can grab them in a hurry."

He swung wide until he could see past the low hills to where the wagons had been halted. Jakes and Shattuck were putting up a rope corral for the extra stock. Tolliver was already getting his orders from Susie.

He went back then for Mellew's horse, taking both animals across the slope and yelling for Susie to come pick them up. Then he had Tolliver within earshot although Jakes was only just starting to run toward him. "You get the orders, Ben?" he asked.

"Got 'em, Cap'n. How long do we hold here?"

"I don't know. Be ready to move back to the wagons if they try to flank us. Give me a chance to try some talk but make any move that seems to need making." He was afoot by that time, leaving the two horses for Susie and running back toward where Mellew crouched in the creek.

He couldn't get the weapons' shortage out of his mind. Jakes was carrying Ben's carbine, leaving the old man with nothing but the captured revolver. Neither of them could provide effective cover fire from the hill. Back at the wagons there would be only Susie and her single-shot carbine. A head-on fight would be plain suicide.

He watched Jakes and Tolliver get into position where a ledge ran across the shoulder of the nearer hill, bushes below it providing a natural screen. From that point they might surprise the attackers in a close-up fight, but they couldn't help much in an attack on the creek.

Hale remained in the open until the outlaws topped the rise. He let them see him and then he took his time about getting down behind the bank of the gulley. The move brought the pursuers to a halt, but after an exchange of talk they came on again.

"We could cut the odds real fast," Mellew grumbled. "Let 'em get close and then cut into 'em."

"Do it my way. I let them see me. They'll come in mighty careful and that's the way I want it."

"Talk won't do a damned bit o' good. Maddigan ain't goin' to take nobody's word for nothin'. If'n he's got it in his craw that I'm haulin' gold there won't be nothin' stop him but a bullet."

"I'll have a try at it. We're in no shape to start a fight."

"We can get just as dead lettin' them start it as with us doin' it. And we could cut the odds some by shootin' first."

"You heard me!" Hale snapped. "Now stay down. They're coming on."

The eight men were bunched as they came down toward the creek. Hale asked, "Know any of 'em except Maddigan? He's the big man, of course?"

"That's him. And I don't know none of the others."

"What about the little man on our left. He's the one who was with Ryan. Any chance that you'd know him?"

"No."

"Then I'd guess that both Ryan and Maddigan recruited somewhere in outlaw country. This gang will be tough."

Mellew grunted again. "Looks like Mad borried some of his stock. From the gun deal, I mean. Every one o' them bastards is totin' a musket."

"We'll keep it in mind. A musket's not the handiest weapon in the world for a man on horseback."

"It won't help. They'll sit tight and hammer us down, outrangin' us the way they do."

That ended the exchange. Both men simply watched as the outlaws came toward them. Maddigan turned to call out low-voiced orders and the others began to spread into a sort of company-front formation. Evidently they proposed to flush the man they had seen go into the creek before they tried anything else. Hale noticed that this gang was made up entirely of white men. Two of them might be mixed bloods or perhaps Mexicans but he guessed that the rest of them were deserters or just plain outlaws. Maddigan had collected a tough crew.

"Remember," he warned Mellew, "don't fire a shot until I give the word."

"You're the boss, damn it! But I'm going to keep this stinkin' musket square on Maddigan. Look what that big bastard's totin'!"

Hale had just gotten a look at the oddly shaped weapon that the big man was carrying in front of him. The sight was not reassuring. Somehow Maddigan had gotten hold of one of those Spencer repeaters that the Yankees had been using so effectively for the past year or so.

"One o' them damned guns they load on Sunday and shoot all week!" Mellew muttered. "He'll give us hell with that thing if we don't get him first!"

"I'll still try talk," Hale told him. "But be

217

ready." A Spencer repeating rifle at fifty yards would be tough to face. It was time to halt the advance before Maddigan could get his repeater into even closer range.

"Hold it right there, Maddigan!" he shouted. "We've got you covered. Let's do some talking before a lot of people get hurt."

Chapter 16

There was a flurry of movement among the men behind Maddigan but the big fellow simply pulled to a halt. At his signal two riders cut to one side but all of them drew six-guns or lifted muskets. They were puzzled, but they were ready. They didn't know how many men were in front of them and they didn't know what to make of the challenge.

"Now you put the fat in the fire!" Mellew growled. "They'll cut us to bits if we make a wrong move now."

Hale ignored him and shouted again. "We don't want trouble so don't start any. You're chasing the wrong people."

Maddigan snapped another order and his men fanned out into something like a line of battle, guns held ready. The big man waited until the formation suited him and then he shouted toward the creek, "I'm listenin'."

"We haven't got what you want," Hale yelled. "No gold. No cartridges. A fight won't get you a thing."

"Who the hell are you?"

"Hale. Captain of Texas Rangers. I've already overhauled one wagon that was supposed to be hauling gold and another loaded with musket cartridges. I've destroyed the cartridges and there's no gold."

"You're a liar! I don't believe you're a Ranger and I ain't takin' nobody's word about that gold. Where's Chris Mellew?"

"With us. We've searched his wagon. There's no gold in it. You're wasting your time—like Lorry Ryan was. Don't get killed for it the way he did."

Maddigan hesitated then but came back with another yell. "If you're a Ranger you and me oughta talk this over. Mebbe we could make a deal."

"I tell you there's nothing in it for you."

"Don't try to tell me, Ranger. I'm the one as ought to be tellin' you. That slippery bastard fooled you. If you're bein' honest with me, that is."

"I'm being honest. I'm telling you not to get people killed on a wild goose chase. And, believe me, somebody is going to get killed if you try to rawhide us." He hoped the threat might make some of Maddigan's men uneasy.

"This ain't no wild goose chase," the big man yelled in reply. "Mellew got the gold outa the ship. I seen it myself, right after Chris knifed the skipper and lugged the stuff ashore. Gold coins. He didn't come out here without bringin' it, I know that much!"

"No jewels?" Hale mocked, stalling for time. "The yarn I heard said it was gold and jewelry and all that kind of thing. Why not make it sound good while you're at it?"

"Listen, Rangerman. I ain't foolin' about this. There wasn't no jools in the box Chris brung ashore. Just coins. Gold money. Now git outa my way and nobody gits hurt but Mellew."

"Why not Garnsey?"

"The hell with *him*. I kin sell the guns all right, cartridges or no cartridges. I want that gold and I aim to git it!"

"I tell you there's no gold in Mellew's wagon!"

"It's there, all right," Maddigan insisted. "Let's make a bet on it, Ranger. You stand aside and let my boys look. Do it peaceful like and we don't bother nobody. That's fair enough, ain't it?"

Hale didn't have a chance to reply. A musket boomed in his ear, the blue smoke rolling out in front of Mellew. The outlaws promptly spread out a little more, guns swinging to open fire on the smoke. Mellew had ended any chance of avoiding a fight.

For a full minute there was nothing to do but to wait and find out what would happen next. Hale kept his head down, staring grimly as Mellew reloaded the musket. He didn't even swear at the stocky man, although he had a feeling that he should curse him for missing if not for any other reason. There was not much question about the reason for the shot. Mellew didn't want Maddigan to do any more talking. He had fired in something akin to panic, not fearing any actual deal between Hale and Maddigan, but trying to keep some piece of information from coming out. And that was a useless sort of gesture, Hale thought; the truth was now pretty obvious.

Then another thought came to his mind. It really didn't make much difference. There could have been no deal with Maddigan. Not only because the big man could not be trusted but also because it would have left the outlaw crowd intact to get on with their gunrunning. The mysterious gold had become the bait that was keeping those guns in a position where there was still some chance of getting to them. Maybe the chance wasn't a very big one but it was still a chance.

The outlaw strategy became apparent as soon as the first rattle of gunfire ended. The enemy raiders were pulling back as they reloaded, taking fresh orders from their burly leader. Without delay they started forward once more, riding straight at the creek crossing but in a different formation. Jed and three other men formed a front rank with Maddigan and three others trailing them by a few yards. As they moved into musket range the front rank opened fire, their timing almost military in the opening volley but then a scattered succession of revolver fire. The whole idea seemed to be keeping the defenders pinned down.

Hale watched anyway, knowing that neither musket or revolver fire would be very accurate under the conditions. He saw the front rank split, two men wheeling toward each flank, to disclose what had happened behind that wall of firing. Maddigan and one of the Mexicans had gone to the ground and were preparing to fire from prone positions, the other men having retreated with their horses. There was a crispness in the maneuver that reminded Hale that he was facing tough enemies. Even before the Spencer began to throw its fifty-caliber slugs at the creek the conclusion was certain; this Maddigan was a good strategist. Moments later Hale knew that the big man was also a good marksman. The Spencer slugs were throwing dirt all over the two men crouching in the creek.

"Why don't Jakes and Tolliver cut loose?" Mellew snarled as he rammed a fresh cartridge into his musket. "We need help!"

"They're too far away," Hale said simply, choking back a lot of angrier comments that he would have preferred to make. This was no time for petty wrangling; all that counted now was to set up some kind of defense against the attack that was forming.

"They're smart," he went on, nodding toward the rattle of firing in front of them. "Maddigan and the other jigger pin us down here while the others ride around us and hit the wagons. They've got to know that the wagons can't be far away, even if they haven't seen 'em yet."

"Why in hell did I have to miss?" Mellew complained. "I had the gun square on the big bastard."

"Too scared to hold steady," Hale told him dryly. "Scared of what Maddigan might tell me."

"Go to hell!"

"Likely enough we all will." He swung to bawl new orders at the men on the hill. "Stay down back there. In a minute Maddigan's going to be reloading. I'll open up with the six-gun. When I do run for the wagon! They'll be needing you back there."

"Got it," Tolliver's voice sounded thinly. "Are ye gonna be all right where ye are?"

"No worse than anybody else. Just do as I say. Mellew can go with you; he's no damned good here."

The stocky man started to growl a reply but Hale cut him off. "Get back there when I give the word. With those flankers divided the way they are you may be able to cut 'em up a mite. Even the odds a little, if possible. Then we could have a chance."

The outlaw fire slackened then and Hale took a quick look. Both men out front were reloading. "Run!" he yelled, raising himself up a little to take fair aim with the Colt. He heard Mellew scrambling out of the creek but he kept his mind on his own problem. A revolver at this range wasn't much of a gun.

His first shot threw dirt just in front of Maddigan so he aimed a little higher. This time he didn't bother about checking results but simply banged away with two more shots. A quick look over his shoulder told him that his companions were making good their retreat so he stopped firing and reloaded. He didn't want to be caught with an empty gun if the men in front of him should change tactics and try to rush him. He actually hoped that they would; in that kind of a fight he could hold his own.

Maddigan wasn't that stupid. He simply remained flat, apparently unhit, slamming away with the Spencer. He must have seen the retreat of the other three men but he didn't waste any slugs on them. His evident intention was to keep Hale down while his men struck at the wagons.

Tolliver was bawling breathless orders by that time, setting up a defense behind the hill. Hale began to feel a little easier. The odds were not going to be too bad back there and the defenders could choose their own positions. Maybe the outlaws had made their first mistake.

Then Maddigan's fire ceased. The Spencer was not empty, Hale knew; he had been counting the shots. Maybe the big man thought that he had kept up the cover fire long enough.

A rattle of gunshots from behind the hill hinted that such was the case. It sounded to Hale as though both flanking pairs had swept in at the same moment, hitting the wagons from two sides. Then the fire ceased and he knew that his guess had not been correct. He took a quick look toward Maddigan and was surprised to see the big fellow and his companion running back toward their horses. Another move was due.

Then Tolliver yelled again, this time in obvious alarm. Hale caught enough words to guess what had happened. The attack on the wagons had been a feint, drawing a bit of fire but ending before it actually amounted to anything. Now both sets of flankers were cutting back toward the creek. Their strategy seemed clear; they were planning to cut off the defender of the creek before they turned their attention to the wagons.

Hale knew that his situation was desperate. Within a matter of seconds he would have enemies driving at him from three separate directions. The creek bank would not shield him against either of the flanking parties so he jumped across to the opposite side, using a clump of willows as a screen. It wasn't much but it was better than being completely exposed to a cross-fire.

He watched as the attack developed, keeping low and quiet. Jed and another outlaw were spurring down on him from the east while Maddigan and his trio drove straight up the wagon trace. The flankers on the west were still hidden by the rising ground but Tolliver's shouting told him that they were attacking. No shots had been fired as yet so he assumed that they hadn't seen him crawl into the willows.

More shouts from the wagons hinted that Old Ben was trying to get help started. He saw Jed and the other man swerve as though to meet an attack, both of them slowing as they swung around. For the moment they were not going to be a serious threat so Hale went back to the cover of the creek bank. It appeared that Maddigan's frontal attack would be the tough part of the deal so the original position seemed like the best bet. He would have to depend on Tolliver to handle the flankers. The big item now was Maddigan and that damned repeating rifle.

This time his move was spotted and the big man opened up. He was not so accurate now. Firing from the saddle was a little different proposition and the Spencer slugs were going wild. Hale didn't expose himself recklessly, but he could still keep an eye on the attack. A couple of bullets threw mud from the damp creek bank as one of the flankers opened fire at long range but Hale didn't pay any attention. He forced himself to ignore that part of the fight, simply waiting for Maddigan and his men to draw within six-gun range.

It didn't take long. Hale realized that the Mexican was slowing his pace so as to steady himself for a good shot. The others would do the same at any moment. He forced himself to ignore the man with the musket and concentrated on the shot that would mean so much.

It took two slugs to do it but Maddigan went down, the Spencer crashing to the ground a dozen feet from him. More shots banged in Hale's rear but he didn't turn his head. One of the outlaws in front was wheeling as though to try for the Spencer. Hale shot him cleanly off his horse. This time he used only one shot.

The Mexican brought his musket to bear then and Hale knew that something was burning at the side of his neck. He fired at the Mexican but the man spurred away, trying to reload the musket as he retreated. The fourth outlaw followed without even trying a shot and Hale let him go. He wanted something left in the six-gun for the enemies who were behind him.

He jumped the creek once more, a sidelong glance telling him that there was blood on his left shoulder. He could still use the left arm and he did not feel more than a numbing kind of pain so he didn't look again. The slug must have barely grazed him at the spot where neck and shoulder met.

He went through the willows as fast as he could travel, not looking for cover now but anxious to take a hand in whatever it was that was happening around the curve of the hill. He slipped in the mud and almost jammed his gun into the slimy mess but somehow avoided that disaster. Then he realized that only one rider was coming up to take the attention of the flankers on that side. It was Susie, her short hair blowing in the wind as she drove in.

He saw that she was riding low on her horse, the carbine held ready. Evidently she had startled them into delaying their attack, but now they were coming on hard, angry at having let one enemy slow them down. Hale opened his mouth to yell for her to back off but he didn't let the words come out. It was too late to stop her now; he might only divert her attention when she needed to keep her wits about her.

He blasted off two shots with the six-gun, knowing that it was a futile gesture. Jed and the other outlaw simply continued the charge, both of them bringing weapons to bear.

Hale fired again, hoping to spoil their aim, but he was too far away. Susie raised the carbine and blazed away almost at the same instant that the two men fired. By that time she was so close to them that the muzzle blasts almost seemed to meet.

Hale was running hard by that time but he knew that he would be too late. Susie and her horse had gone to the ground. Jed hung to the saddle for a second or two but then he tumbled sprawling to lie still. The other man glanced once at Hale and beat a hasty retreat, trying to reload the musket and handle his mount at the same time.

Hale slowed to a walk, knowing that the effort was making him a bit unsteady. There was more blood on his shoulder so he knew that he had to handle himself carefully. He shoved fresh charges into the six-gun, keeping a sharp lookout for more outlaws.

Then he heard Old Ben's voice raised in a new yell of alarm. It sounded as though the old man had been caught out in the open between the wagons and the other flankers. Hale started to turn toward him but then changed his mind. He had to see about Susie first. She had tried to save his life and he didn't propose to desert her now.

He was staggering when he reached her, but managed to steady himself for a quick examination. Her forehead was scraped and there was a swelling beginning to show there but he could see no bullet wound. He pulled her away from the still threshing horse and took another look. She was breathing and her pulse was good. Evidently both outlaws had fired low, hitting the pony but missing the rider. Susie had been knocked out by her headlong fall.

A vast relief flooded through him, but he didn't take time to analyze his own feelings. There was a fight still going on and it wasn't developing as he had expected it would. He had to get back to . . .

Tolliver's shouting became intelligible at that moment. Old Ben was telling him that Mellew had made a break for it and that the surviving outlaws were chasing him. Hale let himself sink to the prairie, trying to keep the dizziness away. For the moment his only reaction was one of some satisfaction. Somehow it seemed like a mighty good idea for outlaws to be chasing Chris Mellew. The farther away they chased him the better!

Chapter 17

He poked gingerly at the neck wound, wincing a little but deciding that it wasn't serious. Getting his wind back eased the dizzy spell and he began to think again. This was no time to get smug over Mellew's troubles. The danger was still present. And that gun shipment still had to be located. Maddigan's death wouldn't relieve the peril of either Indian war or guerilla raids. The guns had to be found and destroyed!

He saw Shattuck coming toward him at a shambling trot, stark tragedy showing in the lined features behind the beard. For the first time Hale thought he understood the man. Shattuck had been harsh with the girl because he was scared to death that she wouldn't be what he wanted her to be. Affection had been behind anxiety and anxiety had been behind harshness. Hale couldn't sympathize too much but he could understand.

"She's all right," he called, trying to reassure the man. "Knocked cold when her horse went down."

Susie opened her eyes at the sound of his voice but for a moment her expression was one of perplexity. Then she propped herself up on one elbow and asked, "What happened?"

"A lot of things. You got Jed and drove off the other man. That saved my bacon for me but they killed your horse and you landed on your head."

"Yo've got blood on yo'," she said, putting her free hand to the bump on her forehead. "How bad is it?"

"Scratch. Don't fuss about it. Feel able to get up now?"

She gave him that smile he was beginning to like so well. "With a mite of help."

"You got it."

Shattuck moved in to help as Hale gave her a hand and the three of them started toward the wagons. Hale had already made sure that both Jed and the horse were dead.

Tolliver met them when they had covered less than half of the distance. His first words were questions about Susie's bump and Hale's wound. Reassured on both points he explained what had happened at the wagons. When the outlaws began their flanking movement a hasty defense had been set up, Tolliver and Jakes taking the west side while Mellew and Susie took the east. Garnsey and Shattuck had no weapons so their job had been to keep the teams from spooking. It seemed like the best arrangement possible but the sudden swing by both sets of attackers had caught them flat-footed.

"I didn't git it at fust," Old Ben complained. "The pair on my side was behind the rise when they changed direction so I didn't know what was goin' on 'til ole Garnsey started squallin'. Then I looked around and seen Susie gittin' into her

233

saddle. Them two bastards on her side o' the attack was in sight, aimin' at the crick."

"Why didn't somebody give her a hand?" Hale demanded.

"It happened too fast. Jakes hollered that we had to cut off the pair in front of us so I hotfooted it out that way. I figgered Mellew would back Susie like I was backin' Jakes but I didn't look back to see if'n he was doin' it. Anyhow, the sonofabitch didn't."

Hale had already spotted a body that he took to be Albert Jakes lying out some distance beyond the wagon. Evidently Susie had not been the only one who had run into real trouble trying to do a job. What he didn't understand was the sight of Garnsey's body on the ground near Shattuck's ox team. "When did Mellew make his run?" he asked quietly.

"Right off, I reckon. Shattuck kin tell ye more about that part. But what about chasin' the bastard? Are ye fit to ride?"

Gunshots had been dwindling away into the distance as Old Ben talked and Hale gestured toward the sound. "Let Maddigan's boys do the chasing for a while," he said indifferently. "No hurry for us now. Did Betsy—Belle—go with him?"

Shattuck rumbled behind the beard. "She was doin' the drivin'. Jumped fast to git in when he run fer the wagon."

"And Garnsey?"

"Mellew hit him over the head with a gun butt to make him let go of the team. Busted his head wide open, looked like." The man's voice was shaky, but Hale didn't think it was a matter of anger as much as delayed shock at having seen Susie go down.

"But Cap'n . . ." Tolliver couldn't seem to understand Hale's failure to get on the trail of the running fight.

"I know, Ben. We ought to be out there. So go ahead. Keep an eye on what happens, but don't let yourself get trapped. I'll be along later."

Tolliver stared. "Are ye feelin' all right, Cap'n? That wound ain't makin' ye giddy, is it?"

Hale started to shake his head but stopped when pain caught him. "I'll be all right," he said with a crooked smile. "Go ahead and see what you can see. I've got a chore or two to handle before I follow."

"Gettin' bandaged, mebbe?"

"Maybe. If Susie will do for me what I wouldn't do for her. And then I'm going back there to pick up that Spencer rifle. If I've got to do any more fighting—and over a skunk like Mellew—I'd like to have that gun in my hands. I'm getting tired of being outgunned in this damned war."

Tolliver's face was a study when he climbed into his saddle. He was amused, puzzled, a little worried, perhaps even a bit suspicious. He couldn't quite figure out why Hale was talking the way he was.

Shattuck made a quick suggestion as Old Ben rode away. "Suppose I git back there and pick up that Spencer you mentioned? I take it it's a gun?"

"Good idea. I'll try to get this wound fixed up while you're doing it. You'll find a couple of dead men about thirty yards beyond the creek. Bring in anything you find of interest on them—and the guns they dropped."

Susie was already bringing out bandages and drawing some water from the barrel on the wagon's side. "Better sit down and take off yer shirt," she told Hale briskly as her uncle climbed to a horse and headed back toward the creek.

He grinned amiably at her. "Wash your face first. There's dirt in those scrapes."

"No hurry about me."

"Stop trying to be polite. I just like to get nursed by women with clean faces."

"Now yo're tryin' to be funny."

"Of course. I feel that way. A cute little gal just kept me from getting killed. Makes a man feel mighty good."

"Fust time anybody eveh tole me Ah was cute," she said softly.

"I'll try to do it more often. Now will you stop gawking and fix up my wound?" He tried to sound very fierce—and failed.

"Ah shouldn't even touch it," she told him, getting into some of the same style of mock belligerence. "Yo' wouldn't take keer o' mah wound when Ah got hurt."

"That was different. I'm not very good at bandaging and yours was a very complicated job. I didn't quite know how to get around . . . certain difficulties."

"Goin' to git smart, are yo'? Ah kin play the same game. Ah'll jest put a bandage around yore neck and pull it up nice and tight."

"Peace," he begged. "Remember that you saved my life. Don't throw it away again."

By the time Shattuck returned with his load of plunder they were on such good terms that Susie didn't even try to put on any act for her uncle. It was noteworthy that the old man also seemed changed. He didn't offer a word of complaint at the way the girl was fussing over the finishing touches on Hale's bandage.

"I cleaned out the good gun purty well," Shattuck reported as he handed the Spencer down from the saddle. "There was dirt in the muzzle but I don't figger it took no other damage."

Hale glanced at the weapon and found that it was in first class order in spite of its crashing fall at the time of Maddigan's death. When Shattuck handed him an ammunition belt half full of the big brass shells and a full box of extra cartridges he could almost forget about the sore neck. He was now better armed than he had ever been before in his life.

He started getting himself ready to follow Tolliver, asking for more information about what had happened in the defense of the wagons. Shattuck could tell him no more than he already knew. Mellew had simply used the critical moment to make his getaway, abandoning Susie when she rode out to help Hale. Garnsey had been killed merely because he was in the way.

"Don't bring him back here," Shattuck warned. "I'd kill him with my bare hands."

"Don't worry. I'll likely not catch him alive. Maddigan's men will see to that."

"How come they're tryin' so hard to get him?" Shattuck persisted.

Hale didn't reply. He was aiming a quick grin at Susie as he eased himself gingerly into the saddle. "Rest up," he told her. "When I get back we'll swap lies about how much we're suffering."

When she made a face at him his grin broadened and he drove out of camp to follow the tracks Mellew's wagon had made. It hurt his neck to ride but somehow he didn't care very much. He wasn't even too worried about those stolen guns. It was pretty nice to feel that finally all the answers had come to him. Answers and other things.

While he stuck with the business of overtaking Tolliver he listened to the occasional bang of a gun well out ahead of him. Mellew hadn't been trapped yet, evidently. Which was something to be said for the man. He was making a run for it with the odds stacked against him. As nearly as Hale could figure out there must be at least four members of Maddigan's gang still alive, all of them hammering away at Mellew and Betsy. One man and a musket didn't have much chance against that kind of attack.

"How far ahead are they?" he asked tersely when he overtook Tolliver.

"Not fur. Less'n a mile. I cut back from the top o' that next rise when I seen that the wagon was cut off. I wasn't about to be no damned hero tryin' to save the bastard."

"Exactly right. Let's go higher and take a look."

When they were high enough to see the distant wagon with its enemies, Hale asked, "How come there's only three riders up there?"

Ben grinned. "Only five started chasin'—which was all that was left after the fight at the crick. One of 'em was wounded. He straggled along behind and gimme a bit o' trouble. I took care o' that, all right. Then they closed in on Mellew kinda brash and he knocked one colder'n hell with a musket shot. So there's three of 'em left and I ain't made up my mind whether they're madder or scareder."

"They're madder," Hale said quickly. "Look at them now!"

"We ain't goin' to git into *this* fight," Old Ben

commented. "It's goin' to be all over. They're drivin' in hard."

At the distance they could see the attack form on three sides of the wagon at the same moment. Mellew shot an outlaw cleanly from the saddle but the other two continued the attack, guns sounding only for another few seconds.

"Time fer us to take a hand?" Ben asked.

"No. This is one fight we could stay away from. Both sides were enemies, you might say."

"Sure—but now they're kinda used up. Mellew killed two of 'em anyhow. Ain't ye goin' to do nothin'?"

"Sure. We're going to ease back out of sight and see what happens next. I've sorta been counting on this."

"For what?"

"Figure it out. They wanted Mellew bad enough to take a lot of risks to get him. Let's keep score on 'em. They started out with nine."

"How do ye know?"

"I don't. But it's a mighty likely number. Six in the gang that set up the ambush. Jed made seven but he wasn't part of the original outfit. They had left somebody with the gun wagons. Two wagons means at least two drivers. I think there was a third man with the guns because they picked up an extra somewhere between the river and here."

"So we had ten of 'em to outfight," Ben said with a show of excitement. "Ye got three back at the crick—with Susie's help. I took care of a fourth one. Mellew accounted fer two more. I reckon the odds ain't so bad now—if'n there ain't but two of 'em left with the gun wagons."

"That's about the way I figure it. Now go on with the guessing. Maddigan must have planned to catch Mellew and then go back for the guns, no matter what the gun deal was by this time. I think the survivors will try the same move. So we keep out of sight and let them lead us to the guns. Right?"

"What about Mellew's wagon?"

"They'll take it with them. Wait and see."

Tolliver was looking puzzled again, but Hale didn't say another word until the dust cloud subsided to the north of them. Then they saw that the Mellew ambulance was making a wide circle to the east, cutting back as though to return toward the ford of the Red River. So far as they could determine, one man was on the driver's seat, three horses trailing on lead ropes behind the wagon.

They kept out of sight, letting the dust settle. By the time the ambulance was opposite their position on its return trip they could see what appeared to be several corpses at the point where the fight had ended. It seemed clear that Mellew had accounted for one more outlaw in the hand-to-hand fighting at the wagon. The lone survivor of the gang was driving away with the wagon, apparently having thrown out the bodies of former occupants at the time that he abandoned his own casualties.

"Better ease back there and take a look, Ben," Hale said quietly. "We don't want to leave any wounded lying around, no matter what we think of them. Keep out of sight. I'll see where this man goes with the wagon."

Tolliver was staring hard at the way the ambulance was zigzagging. "I don't figger he'll git fur, Cap'n. That feller's hurt. Chris Mellew musta been mighty tough when it come to standin' 'em off. Too damned bad he didn't show more grit in the fust part o' the fight."

"Depended on how much he wanted to fight," Hale said shortly. "Get going."

He saw that the ambulance was swinging well to the east and the driver's plan seemed fairly obvious. The man was hurt and alone. He had to get back to where his companions guarded the two wagonloads of muskets. Maybe he wouldn't have bothered if circumstances had been different, but now he had to get help and the gun wagons represented his only chance. He was trying to circle wide enough so that he wouldn't be seen from the site of the first fight by the creek.

Hale got a good look at the way he was operating and then headed back to the Shattuck wagon. It seemed only fair now to let Susie and her uncle know how things were going. There would be plenty of time to catch up with the ambulance later.

To his consternation he saw that two riders were coming across the creek, evidently following the same trail the wagons had used. Susie and her uncle were behind the big wagon, the girl taking dead aim with her carbine even though the two newcomers were making signs of peace. Hale didn't wait to make any guesses although his first thought was that another pair of Maddigan outlaws were moving in. He simply put spurs to his pony and got the Spencer ready for action.

The strangers quickly pulled up, still making frantic signs of peace. Hale swung in toward the Shattuck wagon but before he could aim a question at Susie one of the newcomers bawled, "Captain Hale! McLaws here. Remember me?"

Hale relaxed. He remembered McLaws well enough. The man had been a courier for Hood and later for Johnston. "Come on in," he shouted to him, letting the rifle come to rest across his knees.

They came on gingerly, the leathery looking McLaws throwing a crisp salute as he came to a halt once more. "It's all over, Captain," he announced.

"The war?"

"Yes, sir. Gen'ral Lee surrendered back in April. Got hisself in a bind at a place called Appomatox. Johnston wasn't long in doin' the same thing.

The Yanks caught Jeff Davis rigged out in his wife's shawl. Some of the Texas boys is still holdin' out but they ain't got much to go on. It's all over."

"I'm not sorry. What are you doing out this way?"

"Carryin' messages, as usual. Is this the best trail to the Washita? I'm supposed to find that Peace Commissioner and let him know that he ain't got no authority no more."

"This is the trail," Hale told him. "Anything else I ought to know?"

The other man broke in then. He reminded Hale vaguely of Albert Jakes, a little too well dressed for this part of the country. "I'm Harvey Stokes," he announced. "I'm not official—nobody is right now—but it seemed like a good idea to have somebody out here looking after Texas interests. Peace with the various Indian tribes gets more important than ever." He even talked a little like Jakes.

"I understand," Hale told him. "Headley Stiles sent me out here for that very reason. Good luck."

McLaws shook his head as though annoyed at having been backed out of the conversation. "Another thing," he interrupted. "I'm supposed to warn that peace feller about a man named Garnsey. The polecat's supposed to be out this way to see about handin' out some stolen muskets to the Injuns. Nobody's sure about how he's operatin', but it's a cinch he's up to somethin' dirty."

"Not any more," Hale replied dryly. "Mr. Garnsey is under that blanket on the other side of the wagon."

"What about the guns?"

"That's the next item on the program. I think they're just south of here. Two wagonloads of 'em."

"Damn!" McLaws exclaimed. "We rode right past 'em, I'll betcha!"

Hale nodded. "I sorta expected that they might come on after Maddigan crossed the river. How far back was this?"

"Not more'n a couple o' miles. Who's Maddigan?"

"I'll tell you as we ride. How many men were with the wagons?"

"Just the drivers."

"Good. We won't wait for Tolliver then." He turned to wink at Susie. "Tell Mr. Stokes about the guns, Susie. McLaws and I will see if we can't get this whole mess cleaned up. Come along, Mac. You're carrying a rifle in that boot. Maybe you'll get a chance to use it."

Susie reached for her carbine. "Let me go with yo'. I kin . . ."

"Stay here. Maybe you can help your uncle get some of the dead under the ground. It's bad business to leave evidence of fighting in Indian country."

He motioned for McLaws and spurred his horse toward the Red. It pleased him a little that the lean courier was reluctant. The man obviously would have preferred to stay and help Susie with whatever chores she would be handling.

Chapter 18

Hale told the story in some detail as they rode out across the creek. He even included the part about the Penelope gold but passed it off as just another wild yarn that had caused plenty of trouble without being true. By the time they saw the two freight wagons in the distance McLaws under-stood the situation well enough.

"We'll swing out a little to the right," Hale said. "Maybe those wagons are not what I think they are but I'm about fed up with taking chances. You keep your gun on the driver of the first wagon and I'll do the same for the other fellow. I want both of them on the ground with no weapons handy before I start a search."

"Suits me fine, Captain. I've been shot at enough durin' the past four years to last me fer the rest of my life. Playin' it safe sounds real good."

They were within a quarter of a mile of the two canvas-topped freighters when suddenly the lead driver jumped to the ground and ran back to do some fast pointing and gesticulating to his partner. Then both men ran to saddle horses that had been trailing behind the second wagon. The haste which marked their departure toward the Arbuckle Mountains suggested that Mad

Maddigan hadn't made them teamsters because of any great fighting qualities.

"Gonna be real easy," McLaws chuckled. "No point in chasin' them, I reckon?"

"We'll make 'em think we're trying," Hale told him. "I don't want them getting any ideas about that Mellew wagon. It can't be far away by this time. Let's go."

McLaws understood, Hale having already explained how he had planned to let the wounded outlaw and the Mellew ambulance serve as bird dogs for locating the gun shipment.

They followed the fleeing drivers toward broken country but swung away when Hale caught a glimpse of the ambulance stuck in a small gulley. Again they approached with proper caution and again there was an anti-climax. The wounded outlaw apparently had tried to extricate the team but had collapsed from loss of blood. He was dead when they found him.

"Load him into the wagon," Hale said shortly. "Can't leave dead men lying around in this country. Too much risk of it being misunderstood."

Mellew's special ropes were still in the ambulance so it was no great problem to get the wagon clear. Then, with McLaws taking the reins, they started back toward the abandoned freight wagons.

"This here's the right kind o' fightin' fer me,"

McLaws declared with a laugh. "Only a little work and no bullets flyin' around."

"I'll agree with you if we find muskets in those other wagons," Hale told him grimly. "Right now that's what counts."

They found them.

"So it's going to be more than just a little work," Hale grinned, more relieved than he cared to admit. "I want these guns ruined before we set fire to the wagons."

"Ain't you goin' to try savin' 'em?"

"Not worth the effort or the risk. The big idea is to make sure that they don't get used. Start passing 'em out. We'll knock the hammers off and then load up again. After that we push the wagons together, unhitch the teams, and start a fire. We can call it a sort of peace bonfire."

They sweated it out through the late afternoon heat, finally turning away with the flames beginning to lick at two loads of ruined guns. There had been a few boxes of cartridges with the guns and it seemed likely that the extra ammunition Garnsey had hauled must have been part of the deal. Certainly there had been a planned rendezvous between Garnsey and Maddigan but no one would know just what had been expected to happen then. Probably a payoff as well as the delivery of cartridges. Perhaps a doublecross by Maddigan. It didn't make any difference now.

The cartridges were beginning to sputter in the

flames when the two men rode out of sight with the ambulance and the captured horses. Hale was driving the wagon now, his wound aching after the exertions of the afternoon, but his mind refusing to accept any realization that he had to rest and get the slow but steady bleeding stopped. The only thing he wanted to think about was that the big job was done.

They found the Shattuck wagon where they had left it. Old Ben had come in, reporting that he had disposed of the casualties of the running fight. Betsy Appleby's body had gone into a ravine along with the others, buried by the simple expedient of caving in the bank. Ben had learned a lot of useful little tricks like that in his years on the frontier.

Shattuck had been a little more conventional with his similar chore but he didn't want to talk about it. Stokes had helped and he looked a little sick after the experience. Hale didn't press. A dirty job was done. Nothing else mattered. He simply stretched out and let the others do the talking, refusing Susie's offer to put a new bandage on his wound.

By the time everything had been threshed out conversationally for the newcomers Hale felt better. His neck pained but the bleeding had stopped. He could even get a certain amusement out of the way Susie had been answering some suspiciously significant questions on the part of

Stokes. The man kept hinting for information on the Mellew story and Susie kept making fun of it as just another wild treasure tale. Hale wasn't sure why she was doing it that way but it suited him fine.

Finally he stirred himself to the business of cleaning up final details. "Better agree on a few things tonight," he told Shattuck. "We'll be going in opposite directions tomorrow morning so there's no point in delaying."

"Delayin' what?" the old man asked with open suspicion.

"Dividing up the property that's now in our hands. As the only survivors of the group we're entitled to it—except in the case of stolen horses that will have to be returned to legal owners. I propose to take the horses back with me. I'm going into the cattle business, you know, so stock will mean something to me. Some of the ponies will be claimed, of course, but I'll still be ahead of the game, I think. I'm taking Mellew's wagon along to haul the saddles and gear we've picked up from the various outlaws. By the time I get home I probably won't have any official status because the state government likely won't last much longer than the Confederate one. Maybe it's not a very honest way to set up business capital but the stuff is handy and I might as well take it back and use it. Any objection?"

"Why should I have any? It's your choice."

"I'm not claiming it with any authority, you know. I thought you might use the rest of the stuff in the Mellew wagon. Trade goods ought to bring in something, even the kind Mellew had."

"Suit yourself," Shattuck told him indifferently. "Right now I don't figure to spend much time in Injun trade. The past week's got me full up with this part o' the country. I'm goin' to try for some quick swappin' and then I'll head for some place like Denver. I don't reckon I was cut out for the kind o' thing that happens out here in the wilderness."

"Good idea," Hale approved, his eyes on Susie as he spoke. "One of these days I'll be coming up through the Nations with a herd of cattle, either aiming for new range or for beef markets. It'll be a lot easier to find you in Denver than it would be if you were rambling around the prairie in a trade wagon."

Susie looked around quickly and he grinned smugly at her. Then he went on hastily, "Ben, will you and McLaws get the Mellew stuff moved over into Shattuck's wagon? We'll want to be all set for leaving tomorrow morning."

Hale went across to the ambulance with them, watching by lantern light as they brought out the boxes of trade goods Mellew had stocked. There was little in the wagon except the boxes on their sturdy shelves. Jakes and Garnsey had lost all personal property when the other wagon was swept down in the flood. Neither Mellew nor Betsy had carried much in the way of personal property. When the trade goods were all out the only items left were Mellew's tool box and a bundle of clothing which had belonged to Betsy Appleby.

"Leave the tools," Hale directed. "We might need them. Hand out the female stuff. Susie might as well have it."

He took a quick look as Tolliver handed it to him. Wrapped in a petticoat was a thick wad of money. Union greenbacks. He wondered how many Yankee soldiers had contributed to the hoard.

"Don't talk about it," he warned Tolliver. "I want the girl to have it and her uncle would raise hell if he knew. This kind of money, you know."

He rolled the petticoat up as it had been and went across to where Susie was watching the stowage of the Mellew goods in the big wagon. "Let's talk a bit," he suggested. "Over here."

They moved away from the others and the girl promptly asked, "Was yo' meanin' anything when yo' said yo'd be lookin' us up?"

"Sure. Just in case I happened to pick up another wound I'd be glad to know where I could get bandaged up."

"Ah'm serious. Did yo' mean what Ah'm hopin' yo' did?"

He matched her tone. "I think so, Susie. Right now things are so mixed up that it's hard to tell about feelings—but I'm sure planning to come and find you when I can make it."

"Ah'll be raht easy to find."

"I'm not asking you to wait, you understand. It'll be a long time. Maybe two years or longer before I can get a trail herd together and start north. Nobody knows what'll happen in Texas during that time and I could get all tangled up. But I'm coming."

She seemed to be considering the matter in all seriousness. "Two years, hey?"

"About that."

"Hell! Ah can't git outa the cussin' habit in less time than that. Ah'll be waitin'."

They laughed together and he handed her the bundle. "There's money in there. Keep it for emergencies and don't let your uncle know you have it. He wouldn't think much of money like this."

"Ah'll save it," she promised in a low voice. "Then Ah'll fix myself up real good an' git ready to be a lady."

"Just be yourself," he told her. "Who knows? Maybe you'll wind up being cook for a trail herd or something."

"Mebbe it wouldn't be so bad at that," she murmured. "Not if'n Ah was with the proper trail herd."

• • •

Hale and Tolliver made the Red River crossing a little before dark on the next evening, finding that the spot where Maddigan and his men had forded was now little more than a gravel bar. Early June had dried up the flood in a hurry. Hale began to wonder about taking a wagon and a small remuda back into dry country. Probably he should try to stick near the larger rivers for a while.

He took charge of the cooking when they made camp, finding that camp chores put less strain on the wounded neck than the handling of stock. Old Ben was satisfied with the division of work but he had sulked most of the day as though bothered about something. When supper was over he broke his glum silence to ask, "How come ye was so keerful about talkin' to that Stokes jasper, Cap'n? Ye wasn't right out open and honest with him when gold was mentioned. Do ye still figger there's somethin' in the yarn?"

"I think Stokes was like Jakes. Out here on a decent errand but letting himself get excited by a bit of greed. I didn't want to encourage him."

"Oh. Then there's another thing. How come ye turned that money over to Susie? If ye're still fixin' to git into the drovin' business ye'll need all the cash ye kin lay yer hands on. Like ole Ben Franklin said, 'Any fool what don't think money's important oughta try to borrer some'."

Hale kept his face and voice expressionless. "Did Ben really say that? I thought it was something about a fool and his money making good picking for sharpers."

Tolliver grunted. "Too damned bad ye didn't think o' that sooner."

"Maybe it was a matter of pride," Hale told him in the same flat tone. "I was betting I wouldn't need it."

"What d'ye mean by that?"

"That there's more money for the taking. The gold. You heard what Maddigan said back there at the creek. Mellew had it. He killed the ship's captain to get it. Some time ago I figured out where he hid it. Now I'm betting that I figured right. It's as easy as that. I didn't need the greenbacks."

Tolliver was staring now. "Where's the stuff? Dammit, I looked . . ."

"Just think a bit. Forget about the other wagon at Galveston and start adding up all of the things that happened after Mellew showed up here in the valley of the Red. That wagon of his has been the center of everything."

"But we searched it! Good!"

"When Garnsey's ambulance washed down the river in the flood Maddigan and his gang went to a lot of trouble to pull it out and tear it all apart— because they thought it was Mellew's wagon. They knew it had been rolling around in the river so they couldn't have expected to find any normal load in it. But they still did a lot of hard work on the thing.

"Now think about Mellew's attempted getaway. Maybe he thought we'd kill off enough outlaws to give him a small chance but he wasn't stupid. He knew that the odds were all against him. His only chance was to fork a pony and ride like hell—but he didn't do it. He took the wagon. He knew he didn't have a chance that way but . . ."

"So the gold's in the wagon! Where?"

"Remember how smart Mellew was with tools? Ship's carpenter and all that sort of thing? Would a man like that have had somebody else building a wagon top for him at Galveston?"

"That part I kin understand. The wagon I seen was bait to take attention while Mellew worked on this other one here. But . . ." Suddenly he jumped to his feet. "Damned if'n I ain't figgered it out. Them heavy frames what held his boxes. Two thin slabs with grooves in 'em to hold coins could be fitted flat-to-flat and look like a single piece—if'n a good workman done the job."

"That's how I figured it had to be when I saw Maddigan's gang tearing the Garnsey ambulance apart. Today I looked. It's like you say."

Tolliver stared. "Ye mean ye ain't even looked to see if'n the gold's in them sticks?"

"No. Too many people are still curious about the stuff. Remember how it was with Jakes and

Stokes. I think we'll leave it right where it is until we get it back home."

"But don't ye want to figger . . . ?"

"I can wait to find how much it amounts to. I know how much lumber was made up the way you guessed. There's just a bit more than forty running feet of it in those frames. With one layer of gold coins in each such stick, allowing for solid ends where the frames are fitted that's maybe thirty lineal feet of gold coins, laid edge to edge. Figure a hundred dollars a running foot, a little more if they're twenties, and it adds up real nice."

Tolliver made a move as though to head toward the wagon but then he made a wry face and sat down. "Dammit, ye're always right. I ain't even goin' to look. Anyhow, I don't reckon as it's any o' my business nohow."

"If that's a bid for partnership talk I'm ready. This was your idea in the first place. You lied to me—but that didn't make much difference because that's what I always expect you to do. Anyhow, you started the thing and I finished it. So we're even. Maybe you don't deserve anything after all the mess you got me into but I still figure you're an equal partner. Stiles and I can use another partner with money." He let the grin come as he added the final words.

Old Ben wagged his head dolefully, trying to hide the smile that lurked behind the whiskers. "Even when I git gold I also git hell fer lyin'. Jest like the Good Book says, 'A Prophet don't git no credit when he's crowin' on his own dunghill'."

"One suggestion," Hale groaned. "Whenever you feel like there's a bit of philosophy coming on—just be a silent partner, will you?"

E. E. Halleran was born in Wildwood, New Jersey. He graduated with a Bachelor's degree from Bucknell University in Lewisburg, Pennsylvania, and did postgraduate work at Temple University Law School, Rutgers University where he earned a Master's degree in Education, and the University of Pennsylvania in Philadelphia. He worked as a teacher of social studies at Ocean City High School in New Jersey from 1928 until his retirement in 1949. Halleran began publishing Western stories in magazines, with stories in Wild West, Western Story, and feature articles about Western American history in Big-Book Western. His first novel, *No Range is Free*, was published by Macrae Smith in 1944 and had both commercial and critical success. It was followed that same year by *Prairie Guns* (Macrae Smith, 1944). *Indian Fighter* (Ballantine, 1964) won a Spur Award as Best Western Historical Novel from the Western Writers of America. Halleran's Western fiction is meticulously researched with notable accuracy, both as to the period in which it is set and often populated by historical personalities, while the stories are filled with suspense and fast-paced drama. Among the characters in *Prairie Guns* are Wild Bill Hickok, while he was still a U.S. marshal, and the Indian chieftain Roman

Nose. His characters, both fictitious and historical, appear against backdrops of documented historical events through which the historical characters actually lived, and without any overt attempt to create legends or myths. His descriptive and narrative talent is always such that a reader is instantly swept up by the events of the story and becomes deeply involved with the characters. Among his finest books—always a difficult choice with this author—are *No Range is Free*, *Outposts Of Vengeance* (Macrae Smith, 1945) set during the time of the war with the Miami Indians, and *Winter Ambush* (Macrae Smith, 1954) concerned with the attempt by the U.S. Army to quell a Mormon uprising.

Center Point Large Print
600 Brooks Road / PO Box 1
Thorndike ME 04986-0001 USA

(207) 568-3717

US & Canada:
1 800 929-9108
www.centerpointlargeprint.com